Praise for Tom

"This touching story (coauthored by former *Golden Girls* star White) is filled with scenes that will tug at the reader's heart-strings. The descriptions are vivid, and the details about guide-dog training programs are fascinating."

—*Romantic Times,* regarding *Together*

"Sullivan . . . knows how to spin a captivating yarn, and his can-do enthusiasm leaps off the page as he writes of 'the unlimited capacity of the human imagination.'"

—*Publishers Weekly,* regarding *Adventures in Darkness*

"Coming-of-age tales like this one don't come along every day . . . Don't miss this one."

—*The Saturday Evening Post,* regarding *Adventures in Darkness*

Other Books by Tom Sullivan

FICTION

Together (with Betty White)

NONFICTION

If You Could See What I Hear

You Are Special

The Leading Lady (with Betty White)

Special Parent, Special Child

Seeing Lessons, 14 Lessons I've Learned Along the Way

Adventures in Darkness

CHILDREN'S BOOKS

Common Sense

That Nelson

Adventures in Darkness, children's version

aliveday

Tom Sullivan

THOMAS NELSON
Since 1798

NASHVILLE DALLAS MEXICO CITY RIO DE JANEIRO BEIJING

Published in Nashville, Tennessee. Thomas Nelson is a registered trademark of Thomas Nelson Inc.

Thomas Nelson, Inc., titles may be purchased in bulk for educational, business, fund-raising, or sales promotional use. For information, e-mail SpecialMarkets@ThomasNelson.com.

Scripture quotations are taken from the King James Version of the Bible. Public domain.

This novel is a work of fiction. Any references to real events, businesses, organizations, and locales are intended only to give the fiction a sense of reality and authenticity. Any resemblance to actual persons, living or dead, is entirely coincidental.

Library of Congress Cataloging-in-Publication Data

Sullivan, Tom, 1947–
Alive day / Tom Sullivan.
p. cm.
ISBN 978-1-59554-457-5 (softcover)
1. Blind—Fiction. 2. Disabled veterans—Fiction. 3. People with disabilities—Fiction. 4. Labrador retriever—Fiction. 5. Human-animal relationships—Fiction. I. Title.
PS3569.U35925A79 2009
813'.54—dc22 2009014656

Printed in the United States of America

09 10 11 12 RRD 6 5 4 3 2 1

To the men and women of our armed forces who guarantee our freedom with their blood, sweat, tears, and if necessary, with their lives. Thank you.

prologue

The Marine sergeant stared straight ahead, his body ramrod straight as he marched down the white hospital corridor. His distinctive uniform of dress blues signaled a ceremonial occasion, as if he were on a parade ground under review by the adjutant general of the Marine Corps. The scarlet stripe, a reminder of the sacrifices made by his comrades, seemed to punctuate the soldier's mission, one that was far more important than parade ceremony. Cradled in his arms was a box containing something sacred to the morale of the Corps.

Arriving at the patient's door, he waited until the nurse signaled him in. Then he entered the hospital room and, after carefully shifting the package to his left hand, came to attention and saluted the man in the bed.

"Sergeant Johnson reporting by order of the commander, sir." The Marine's staccato voice echoed in the small room.

The patient attempted a smile through swollen lips. "Thank you, Sergeant," he said.

The sergeant placed the box on the bedside table. Sensing the man's hesitation, the sergeant asked, "Permission to open it for you, sir?"

The patient nodded slightly, and the sergeant opened the package.

Inside was a small cake with one candle.

"May I light it, sir?" the sergeant asked.

The patient looked at the cake for several long seconds. Then he leaned his head back and mumbled, "Go ahead, Sarge."

The Marine produced a lighter. When the candle was lit, he announced, "Happy Alive Day, sir."

The patient in the bed painfully raised his right arm and saluted.

chapter one

The dog stilled in his morning walk, watching as a seagull soared overhead. His eyes followed as the bird moved almost imperceptibly, maintaining a position in the wind two hundred feet above the glassy waters of Puget Sound. The panorama of beautiful Bainbridge Island, ten miles long and five miles wide, stretched out before him. The sun was gradually overcoming the thick fog. As the light touched the seagull, the gray wings and white body took on a hue of sunrise pink.

As Brenden McCarthy stretched his muscles, he heard the seagull's cry as it streaked through the sky. The dog looked on as Brenden reached skyward, reminded of another bird's cry up in the Rocky Mountains eight years ago. A sound that had caused him to break his concentration while climbing, slip on loose scree, and begin the steep fall that had resulted in his becoming blind.

But on this remarkable morning in this beautiful place, he realized that the memory was no longer painful. He was a clinical psychiatrist, and his medical training suggested to him that he was now a well-adjusted human being. Then he smiled as he considered that *well-adjusted* was not exactly the right term to describe him. What he was, at long last, was happy and content.

His wife, Kat—or Kathleen when she signed their checks—was his best friend, lover, and confidante. And their two children—*Wow,* he thought—they were gifts from God. Brian was now six, a strapping boy with unlimited curiosity and energy. And then there was his Mora, age four—a daddy's girl all the way. Just hearing her say "Daddy" melted his heart and made him a sucker for anything she wanted. He knew he was turning her into a princess, but so what? Wasn't that the right of all fathers of little girls?

Like the twenty-three hundred other residents of Bainbridge Island, Dr. Brenden McCarthy and his family had moved here for the outdoor lifestyle and easy commute by ferryboat to Seattle, Poulsbo, and Bremerton. Just east of the Kitsap Peninsula and west of the city of Seattle, the island was largely protected by Puget Sound and Port Orchard Bay.

Brenden completed his morning push-ups—one hundred without stopping—and wasn't even breathing hard. *It's great to be alive,* he thought. He had walked the hilly section of the island this morning, strengthening his quads for the upcoming Chilly Hilly bike race he and his wife would compete in on their specially built tandem.

As Brenden stretched, his big black dog, Nelson, stood on his hind legs and surprised his master with a kiss right on the mouth, causing Brenden to laugh out loud. He reached out, found the animal's jowls with his hands, and stretched his fingers to give the dog a friendly behind-the-ears scratching. From the sound of his thumping tail, Brenden knew Nelson appreciated the gesture.

Nelson had completely changed Brenden's life, allowing him to be reborn, in a sense—to create a new life for himself after the accident that stole his sight. Their interdependence fulfilled both man and dog and made them an excellent team.

Brenden knelt down and took the time to study his friend with his hands, patting him all over. He loved the grainy texture of Nelson's fur. Stroking him from head to tail, his sensitive hands glided softly over the animal's body, revealing each contour. But when he reversed the process, rubbing against the grain of the short, wiry fur, Brenden was reminded of when he used to play golf with his father and how a green could be very different when you putted, based on the contour of the grass.

Now his fingers perused the animal. His friend's large head and powerful neck gave the man a sense of the dog's strength and energy. Unlike many Labs, Nelson was in great shape and hadn't developed the boxy, squat body that characterized the typical Labrador retriever in middle age. In fact, Nelson had entered the age of retirement for most guide dogs, but his good health, infinite energy, and exceptional skills kept him working. And Brenden hoped he and Nelson would be a team for more years to come.

Leaning a little closer to Nelson, Brenden took in the dog's smell, which he had come to love, though it was a somewhat sour and salty aroma. Since his sight had been taken away, Brenden had gained an ability to distinguish the slight nuances of various smells. Nelson's scent might be considered foul to some people, but to Brenden the smell related specifically to Nelson and was an element that enhanced their bond.

Even though he knew his sense of smell was heightened, he considered how much better Nelson's olfactory acuity must be. His canine friend could always find him, no matter where he was, just by using his nose. If the animal had been outside playing with the children, when he came indoors he didn't have to go from room to room looking for his master. Instead, he just sniffed the air and went right to the spot where Brenden was—working or resting or watching TV.

Again he hugged his friend, eliciting a big doggy sigh of contentment and pleasure. *What a good team we are,* Brenden thought. "You've got a few more minutes, pal," he told the animal. "I need to do a little more stretching before we head home. You go run on the trails a bit, okay?"

He heard the dog's chain rattle as he shook himself and then took off, but not so far that Brenden lost the sound of his jingling collar. A vigorous morning workout had been part of their daily routine together after getting out of guide dog school, and probably because this morning activity gave Nelson an outlet for his energy, he never broke the rules, even off the leash.

A minute or so later, the dog tensed, drawn to a rustling in the bushes. The black Lab searched the bushes eagerly as if saying, *Ah, someone to play with!* Nelson bounded toward the creature, hoping it would run and giving off a high-pitched bark of pleasure, ready to play a game.

Too bad that wasn't what the skunk was thinking. Assuming his position, with tail facing the charging dog, the skunk let go, hitting Nelson with the pungent spray and eliciting a howl of shock and awe. How could he be so poorly treated by another animal? The big dog ran to his master. Brenden groaned at the smell and feverishly tried to avoid contact.

"Now you've really done it," Brenden said, laughing. "And I still have to walk home with you, you smelly beast. This is a real test of bonding."

Brenden held his breath as he put on the dog's harness and leash, nearly choking as he got up close and personal with the "eau de skunk." It was so bad that he could hear Nelson snorting, as if he was trying to avoid smelling himself.

"I don't know what we're going to do," Brenden said. "Let's see if we have some tomato juice or vinegar at home. If not, you may be living outside for a while, pal."

Even though neither man nor dog could stand the odor, it didn't change the fact that Nelson was extremely careful—flawless in his work—as he began to lead his master toward home, watching the ground to avoid tree roots or other obstacles that might trip up Brenden.

It took them about fifteen minutes to get back to the house. During their trek home, Brenden tried to put his thoughts on anything other than the asphyxiating odor emanating from the black Lab. He considered that in a few hours, as on all workdays, he would be seeing psychiatric patients with problems that, for the most part, were manageable or routine. Sometimes he wondered if he really was making a difference in what some would describe as his "cushy" medical practice. Prescribing routine medications to remedy sleep disorders or to break a guy's smoking habit didn't require a lot of brainpower. True, there were patients who required all his skill as a psychiatrist as they battled the emotional and physical complexities of a more serious problem, such as bipolar disorder or anorexia. Yet he had a nagging sense that something was missing in his work as a psychiatrist. What was it?

His thoughts wandered as the big dog moved him expertly toward home. *I chose to be a psychiatrist,* he reminded himself, drifting into ruminations he had gone through many times before. Before his blindness, Brendan had completed medical school and was just beginning a residency as an orthopedic surgeon, but after losing his sight, he gave up that career—and almost gave up on everything else. But because of the lifesaving counseling he had received, Brenden decided to become a counselor himself. *I chose this profession because I wanted to make a difference in the lives of my patients. But maybe somewhere inside—somewhere deep down in my own psyche—I believe my work should be focused on a specific mission.*

Brenden realized with a shake of his head that though his own experience lent itself to helping people with physical disabilities, he was not prepared to take that on. He hated himself for thinking it, but he just didn't want to be involved with the handicapped. He still did not see himself as one of them. He wasn't like them—those people. He simply wasn't one of *them*.

And yet, as he felt Nelson pull on the harness, he knew he was lying to himself. He was *blind*, wasn't he? Of course he was one of them. So maybe his current medical practice was not the best use of his talent because it lacked mission. Did his focus on patients with relatively easy-to-cure problems, instead of the messier, more complex psychological issues of patients with physical disabilities, make him a fake psychiatrist? Or even more disconcerting, a phony person?

His reverie was interrupted as he became aware that Nelson was pulling aggressively on his arm, indicating some particularly bad road surface in their path. Circumventing the problem, the big dog skillfully moved his master back to the right and continued their walk without even the slightest misstep.

"Good boy," Brenden said. "You may stink, but you're still the best, Nelson." Brenden smiled as he remembered that Nelson's trainer, Smitty, had described the Lab as "the best dog" he ever taught. In thirty years, Smitty had never seen a dog absorb concepts as quickly as Nelson. The lovable Lab had showed exceptional intelligence and focus when applying himself to his work, but—as Brenden found out soon enough—he also displayed a hyperprecociousness when not on duty. The first night that Nelson stayed with Brenden, the dog had chewed up his shoes, socks, and shirt. Brenden, still new to his blindness and unconvinced of his need for a guide dog, had been furious—but it was anger over his personal loss, misdirected toward Nelson.

He later learned from Smitty that Nelson's sensitivity could turn to anxiety if he was in an uncomfortable environment. Though he was perfect when doing his job in harness, Nelson had displayed destructive habits with his prior two masters, neither of whom gave Nelson adequate ways to release his energy or anxiety when he was off duty. Neither of whom had been able to bond with Nelson the way Brenden had.

As they walked, Brenden said a prayer of thanks for his furry friend. He was also grateful for all the smells and textures that permeated the air. Thankfully the island still possessed some beautiful cedar, even though much of it had been cut down in the early days to supply masts for seagoing ships. The sensory blend of sea life coupled with cedar and pine, along with breakfast being cooked by early-morning risers, made for a welcome interruption from the skunk's assault.

Passing Battle Point Park, Brenden decided to forgo his sit-ups, knowing that if he lay on the grass, Nelson would stand over him like he always did, licking his face. The idea of being so close to the dog's pungent odor was too much to stomach.

The dog's tail was rhythmically banging his master's leg as they passed along the edge of the park.

"I know what you're saying, boy. You want to go swimming, and maybe that would be the ticket to getting rid of the smell. The ocean heals everything, you know, but it is still much too cold for me. You might be able to handle it with your fur coat, but it's too cold for your master, so let's just go home, okay, pal?"

Brenden felt the animal's head turn for one more longing

look out at the bay, but Nelson did not break his gait as they continued toward home and family. Then the dog picked up his pace as they crested a rise and started downhill to the McCarthy condo.

Brenden and Kat had purchased a unit on the top floor of a beautiful complex directly across from Eagle Bay. Every day Brenden and Nelson commuted on the Washington Ferry to his clinical practice in Seattle. They both loved the peaceful experience of the crossing, and also appreciated that with no traffic on the Sound, the ferry was always on time.

Nelson pressed his nose on the button for the elevator, and in seconds they were turning left with the big dog's tail once again banging Brenden's leg in anticipation of seeing his family.

When he thought about it, Brenden was amazed at Nelson's capacity to compartmentalize his life and his responsibilities. On the one hand, when he was working, his focus could not be broken. Kat said you could see it in his expression. She often joked that she wished human beings could focus in the way Nelson did. He missed nothing with any of his senses, and his keen awareness gave Brenden the confidence to believe that their team would always be able to work out any problem presented. On the other hand, when Nelson was with the children, he became the ultimate family pet. Brenden had come to understand what differentiated the two Nelsons: it was the harness. When the harness was on, Nelson was on duty, working and serious; but when it was off, the big black Lab loved just being a dog.

As they turned down the hall from the elevator, Brenden

speculated that his family might already smell them coming, and he wondered what kind of greeting they would get.

As Brenden put his key in the lock, he heard the sound of little feet rushing to greet him. Pushing open the door, Nelson did what he always did—burst forward to relish the affection from the family he loved. Then Brenden heard a unanimous response from both children and Kat. "Eew, what smells?"

"It's Nelson," Brenden said sheepishly. "He got sprayed by a skunk."

"It's gross, Dad," Brian said. Mora just held her nose, and practical Kat was already going to the pantry to see if they had any tomato juice or vinegar.

"Okay, team," Brenden said, "we've got to try to get Nelson ready for me to take to work. Brian, you go fill up the tub with warm water. Mora, see if you can find your bottle of children's shampoo. Kat, is there anything else we might use?"

"We have some tomato juice," Kat said.

"Okay," Brenden said. "Let me take Nelson outside, and I'll start with that."

Over the next few minutes, the McCarthy family got busy. Brenden poured tomato juice all over Nelson and—to Nelson's annoyance—rubbed it into his coat. But all that seemed to do was make the smell stronger.

When the tub was ready, the family moved back inside, and Brenden lifted Nelson over the edge and dropped him into the warm water. Now, for a Lab, that was about as good as life gets; he was being patted and stroked and loved, and he was in water. Life couldn't get any better, could it?

The entire family got wet as the big animal enjoyed his bath, shaking water all over the place, soaking the bathroom floor. Rub and scrub and scrub some more. Everybody took a turn, with Nelson apparently finding the whole experience fantastic.

Eventually, after using three or four big towels, Nelson was dry, and the smell had diminished somewhat.

"I don't know," Kat said. "If you bring that dog to the office, I'm pretty sure you'll lose patients."

"Yeah," Brenden said. "I've been thinking about that. I might just have to"—he paused—"get out the old white stick."

"What stick, Daddy?" Mora asked.

"It's called a cane, Mora. I know you've never seen me use it, but it's something that many blind people use to help them get around."

"A cane?" the little girl asked again. "Is it alive? Is it an animal?"

Brenden laughed. "No, princess; it's just a stick."

That's how Brenden had always seen a cane—as a stick, a symbol of limitation, a badge of blindness. He had hated using it in rehab, and the idea that he might have to use it today made him irritated at Nelson, and the realization made him disgusted with himself. It wasn't the dog's fault he got sprayed by a skunk, and didn't millions of blind people use their canes every day?

Suck it up, McCarthy. Just suck it up and stop feeling sorry for yourself.

"Listen," Kat was saying, "I'll get the kids to school while you take a shower. Your clothes will be laid out on the bed. And

I'll give you a sharp tie so you don't feel uncomfortable with the cane."

She knows me so well, Brenden thought. Her instincts had always been pitch-perfect, but she had never been a docile spouse. When he needed it—and he often did—she was not afraid to tell it like it was.

They had met while Brenden was rehabilitating from his accident. Kat was a ski instructor in Winter Park, Colorado, at the National Sport Center for the Disabled, and they had fallen in love during their time together on the slopes. When they were dating, Kat used to tease him that being blind wasn't such a bad thing because he didn't know how ugly she was. In truth, Kat Collins-McCarthy was a stunner whose smile could light up the world and whose eyes were so lively that people couldn't stop looking at her. She stayed in great shape, and even though Brenden met Kat after losing his sight, he could tell she was a babe. But her guileless sense of her own self-worth added to her charm, and Brenden loved her for her goodness, honesty, and that quality of innocence that made her an extremely positive person.

Brenden knew he could not live without Kat because their love was special in so many ways. Principal among these was the directness of their communication and the trust they had established—much in the way he had with Nelson—in developing a relationship that could best be categorized as interdependent.

He knew the pride she took in dressing him just so, shopping mostly at an exclusive men's store in Seattle called Mario's, where she spent much too much money. But she was committed to the idea that if he looked the part of a professional, people would be more willing to accept the concept that Dr. Brenden McCarthy was a competent psychiatrist, rather than merely a blind one.

He understood that Kat was determined to make his blindness only one part of how people saw him. In his mind he was Brenden McCarthy—husband, father, psychiatrist, athlete, and citizen of the world—who happened to be blind. He knew that he couldn't eliminate his disability, but he was driven to express his abilities rather than live in his disability.

KAT WAS BACK FROM taking the children to school by the time Brenden had showered and dressed. As her husband came down the stairs, she smiled to herself at how handsome he looked. She saw him go to the closet and rummage around behind the winter coats to find his white cane. She watched as he unfolded it, clicking the pieces together.

"Honey," she asked carefully, "do you want me to walk you across to the ferry? I mean, can you do that with your cane?"

"I'd better be able to," Brenden said. "I do it every day with Nelson."

Kat almost answered, *But that's different,* but she bit her tongue to stop herself.

"Okay," she said lightly, "then give me a hug and get out of here."

Nelson was already at the front door, skunk smell and all, waiting for Brenden to put on his harness and leash.

"I'm sorry, boy," the man said. "You're going to have to stay here with Kat."

The big dog started whining. He ran to his master, turned, and then went to the front door again, expectant.

"I'm sorry, Nelson," Brenden said again. "Stay, boy. Stay with Kat."

He turned to his wife. "I think you'll have to hold him until I'm out the door. He doesn't understand."

Kat took the big dog by the collar and put him in the guest powder room with the door closed.

"Okay," she said again. "Good luck."

"Thanks. I'll need it," Brenden said, and he couldn't have been more right.

THERE ARE TWO TECHNIQUES Brenden would utilize as he moved through space with a cane—the inside and outside applications. When inside a building, a blind person is taught to put the cane across the body, tracking the wall in a corridor or hallway to find a door or an elevator or a flight of stairs. Outdoors, the cane is tapped from side to side, swinging left as the right foot moves forward and right when a corresponding left step is taken.

To Brenden, all of this was mechanical, arduous, and cumbersome. Whereas Nelson moved quickly and could think them through the travel process, Brenden was now forced to remember how many steps it was to the elevator from their apartment. How many steps to walk down after opening the front door and exiting the building. Where exactly was the crossing that would lead to the ferryboat dock, and once there, where in the world was the ticket counter?

A trip that normally took Brenden and Nelson just two minutes took ten with the cane, and he found himself becoming impatient and irritable.

Boarding the boat, he was nervous about feeling the gangplank with the tip of the stick. Nelson always took him right to an empty seat, but now, as he groped for a place on one of the benches, he kept sticking his cane into people's feet.

"Hey, Doc, where's Nelson?"

"Where's the pooch, Doc?"

Brenden tried to answer everyone politely, but he found himself becoming anxious as the ferry made the twenty-minute crossing and docked in Seattle.

THE BIG BLACK DOG was also becoming anxious. For Nelson, the idea that his master had left without him was unusual. Oh sure, Brenden and Kat occasionally went out at night, leaving Nelson with the children and a babysitter, or took their bike rides without him, but this was different. It was different because the man had dressed to go to work, and work was what Nelson did. He had gone upstairs to Brenden's office, where he always waited for his master, but now he was feeling a vibration, some honed instinct cultivated by great animals who had served their owners over thousands of years.

He ran downstairs and scratched at the front door. Kat tried to settle him and finally put him back in the office with the door closed. The dog was whining now, almost howling with concern, and Kat wasn't sure how to handle it. When she tried to pat him and tell him everything would be all right, it only enhanced his efforts to express to her that he was worried.

So what to do? She decided that the best course of action was to leave Nelson alone, and that drove the dog into action. She was in the laundry room, folding clothes, when she heard the screen in the open window crash; Nelson leapt through the upstairs window, landing hard but bounding up and galloping away in the direction of the dock and the ferry he believed must have carried Brenden away.

"Oh no, Nelson!" Kat cried as she raced to the front door, picked up his leash, and ran after the concerned guide dog.

BRENDEN KNEW THAT IT was thirteen blocks straight up Marion Street from Pier Fifty-two at the Seattle dock to his office in the Swedish Medical Center. He had chosen the center because the campus of Seattle University offered him easy access to its library for any supplemental materials he might need to provide better patient care.

The walk was basically uphill, and there would be crossings at Western and Post, followed by First through Ninth, then Terry Street and Bourne Avenue, and then he would find himself directly in front of the Swedish Medical Center complex.

On the surface, easy. With Nelson, a piece of cake. But on

this morning, with only the white stick to guide him, potentially disastrous. Between Sixth and Seventh Streets, Brenden and Nelson would enter an underpass because of the freeway running above them. The noise level was always high, but the competence of the dog and the trust the man had in the animal made the transition easy.

Why? Brenden wondered. *Why on this day are there repairs going on inside the underpass?*

Men were working with jackhammers, and evidently there was a temporary barrier—which Brenden's cane and then his shins found—placed there for people to find an alternate route back onto Marion Street. Not able to see the detour sign, Brenden was completely confused, and there was no Nelson to ask for help. Disoriented by the cacophony, he turned the wrong way, tripping off the sidewalk and turning his ankle. The pain, the embarrassment, and the reality of his blindness came crashing in on him with a profound intensity he hadn't felt since early in his rehabilitation. As he struggled to clamber back to his feet, a burly construction supervisor rushed over to help.

"Dude," he said. "What are you doing out here like this? I mean, you being . . . uh, I mean . . ."

"You mean blind, sir? Right now I'm asking myself the same question. Look, would you mind giving me some help to get around the construction? I think I can do the rest."

There was that awful awkwardness as Brenden and the man tried to decide how to walk together. Brenden worried that the guy was going to get a couple of his big buddies and carry him like a potato sack, but eventually Brenden got hold of the man's arm and followed him, limping, back onto Marion Street.

From there, every crossing was awkward and nerve-racking. Brenden had almost forgotten how to listen to traffic flow because Nelson had taken care of that concern for the past eight years. Eventually he tapped his way into the Swedish Medical Complex, though he had all kinds of trouble finding the elevator.

As before, someone was there to help, pushing the fourth-floor button for the Madison Tower, and he finally arrived in his corner office, collapsing gratefully into his chair with a cup of coffee delivered to him by Janet, the secretary a number of the doctors shared.

WHEN KAT ARRIVED AT the dock, she could not see the black Lab, but she heard the commotion coming from the waiting ferryboat. As she arrived at the gangway, she saw Nelson literally running between people's legs, his nose to the ground, smelling, searching for his master. The ferry passengers were pointing to the dog and saying things like, "Where did that dog come from?" and "Wait, isn't that the blind guy's dog?"

"Excuse me," Kat said to the young crew member standing at the edge of the gangway. "That's my dog, Nelson. He ran off, probably thinking my husband would be on the ferry. I'm sorry about that. May I go on board and get him?"

"Sure," the man said. "I know your dog. I've seen him ride with your husband a few times. Go ahead, ma'am."

As much as the big animal loved Kat, getting him to leave the boat without his master wasn't easy. What was critical to Nelson was that he find Brenden, or at least that he satisfy himself that his master wasn't on the boat.

Other passengers got involved in the game, as if they were chasing a greased pig. Eventually two men cornered Nelson, and Kat got a leash on him and led him back home, where she kept him firmly tied to a chair, even though the smell from his earlier encounter with the skunk nearly choked her to death.

As he waited for his first patient, Dr. Brenden McCarthy considered the significance of his relationship with his big black guide dog. He realized that Nelson not only had changed his life but had become indispensable to him. The dog made Brendon's career—and livelihood—possible. Even though Nelson's high-strung personality off duty sometimes challenged the McCarthy family's patience, they received so much unconditional love from the pooch that any rowdy behavior was accepted as part of the package.

His cell phone rang abruptly.

"Hello," he said.

"Well, your pal really went crazy this morning," Kat told him.

"What happened?" Brenden asked.

"Oh, nothing much. Nelson just jumped through an upstairs window, broke a screen, ran across the street, got on the ferry, and almost escaped to Seattle trying to find you."

"Oh my," Brenden said, not able to hide his smile. "I guess that dog loves me."

"Ya think?" Kat said.

chapter two

I go for mine; I got to shine.

Now throw your hands up in the sky.

Kanye West is pumping through the boom box. The boom box, with its ten-inch woofer, bounces the sound off the nearby tenements, and the word *shine* has an echo that amplifies the macho essence of the game.

It's the courts in Laurel Park, at the corner of Laurel Street and Center Avenue, Compton, California. The game is "you stay, you play." Hold the court, and you play; lose, you're a dog, leaning on the fence with your arms crossed in an attitude that says, *I'm better than anyone here if I want to be.* Crips and Bloods own this turf, but here on the courts, gang is put aside for the game.

It's early evening, before the lights come on. The heat of the August day and the sweat of the men rise into the air, mixing with the LA smog to create an acrid, moist heaviness that envelops the game, holding everyone in the vortex, focusing their effort.

Kanye is continuing to rap about the good life and getting it all for free, no matter where you are—from New York to Atlanta, Miami to right here in LA.

The teenager is compact, powerful, a force of energy, one with the basketball. He moves not with the grace of a dancer, but with the darting intensity of a small animal who knows he has to be quicker and smarter just to be in the game.

They're playing twenty-by-ones, and you have to win by two. There are no foul shots in the game. When a foul happens, you play on, because the crowd is your jury. There are no refs and no rest. He slides behind a teammate's pick and elevates. The boy has hops as he hangs in the air, and the jump shot is pure.

Swish. The net doesn't even move.

His teammates appreciate it. "Dog," one yells, "that is NBA!"

"A Kobe," another chimes in, meaning Kobe Bryant of the Lakers.

"Hollywood, dog," a third adds. "Big-time Hollywood."

Now he's on defense. *Never watch a head fake,* his coach has taught him. *Head and shoulders mean jack. It's all below the waist. Knees and hips. Slide. Slide. Keep your feet under you. Don't leave your feet. Stay down. Hands up. Watch the ball. Don't get screened off. Anticipate the pass.*

Yes! His instincts are right, and he steals the ball. He's out in front, flying down the court, and although he's small, he gathers himself just inside the foul line. Knees flex, now soar. He's in the air, cradling the ball, and somehow he's above the rim ready to rock the baby. A slam dunk right over the biggest dude on the court. It's a sure thing.

But it doesn't happen. Instead, he's hanging in the air, suspended in space, unable to find the ground, unable to feel his feet, unable to come down because . . . because . . .

HE SCREAMED, HIS DREAM becoming the ultimate nightmare as reality brought him crashing to earth. He could not feel his legs. He could not feel his feet. When his hands reached out and touched his knees, he could not feel them. He clawed at them, digging his nails into his skin until he bled, willing himself to feel. But there was no feeling, and the knowledge that he was paralyzed from the waist down caused him to scream again, bringing the nurse and the shot and the tortured sleep that he wished could be death.

Better to have died when the IED exploded than to live like this, Antwone Carver thought as the drug-induced sleep took over. *Better to be dead.*

WHEN HE AWOKE AGAIN, the nurse was standing over him. She looked down to read the hospital bracelet. "I'm Ms. Anderson," she said. "And you're Antwone Carver?"

He did not nod, but his eyes said yes.

"Well, Mr. Carver, I'm here to clean you up. How about a shave and a nice sponge bath?"

The young Marine didn't respond, so she took that for a yes.

She brought the bed to a sitting position, filled a metal bowl with warm water, and began to shave him. Antwone noticed she was really good at it, perhaps because she had performed this task many times on guys who couldn't do it for themselves. He did not answer any of her questions, nor did he make eye contact with her, even though she was quite pretty.

Finishing the shave, she emptied and refilled the bowl and then began to sponge him down. This was more than he was willing to accept.

"Just leave me alone, will you, ma'am?" he asked, turning his head away from her. "Just leave me alone."

"I can't do that, Corporal Carver. I've been told you have a visitor, and we want you looking your best."

A visitor? Antwone's eyes finally found her face. "Who's here to visit me?"

"Oh, I think it's someone you'll want to see." The nurse smiled knowingly. "In fact, I know it's someone you'll want to see. A very beautiful woman. I think I heard her name is Darla."

Darla. The sound of her name caused the young man's upper body to jump. "Darla's here?" *My Darla is here.* His voice quavered. "Does she know? I mean, has anybody told her that I'm . . ." The words stuck in his throat, and the young nurse, seeing his face, tried to help.

"You mean does she know that you've had a spinal injury?

Yes, I believe someone has talked to her, so let's get you cleaned up. We don't want to keep a beautiful woman waiting."

Feeling a little desperate, Antwone said, "Ma'am, when you finish . . . I mean, when you finish cleaning me up, could you help me get dressed?"

"I don't know, Corporal Carver. That's unusual, considering your condition."

"Listen. I've been going to therapy. I mean, they move me around and stuff. What's the matter with me can't get any worse. Just help me put on my uniform, please. I want . . . I want my wife to see me as a man, a Marine."

The nurse smiled. "Okay, Corporal," she said, "I'll get some help, and we'll get you all spit and polished."

"Spit and polished" was a long way from how Antwone Carver grew up. Born in South Central LA, in a family of eight with no knowledge of his father, Antwone hovered on the edge of a life in the gangs. His mother, Ruthie, did the best she could to raise her children with moral and Christian values, but the streets and peer influence are powerful things. Antwone spent some time in juvie for shoplifting before good fortune smiled: a U.S. Marines recruiter came to his high school and was impressed with the kid's skills on the basketball court. The next time Antwone got in trouble for stealing a car, he remembered the recruiter, and a deal was made with the courts allowing Antwone to take early enlistment in the Corps and ship out to Parris Island for basic training. *Esprit de corps*, some call it. The drill sergeants call it "getting right." It's when a young man crosses over and decides that the Corps is his family.

That's what happened to Antwone Carver. Over the next three years, even after one tour with Desert Shield during the incursion into Iraq, Carver decided he would be a lifer, expecting to be a sergeant major with a big pension and security.

Returning home after Desert Shield and waiting for his next assignment, Corporal Carver was billeted at Camp Pendleton in San Diego. And there, in a club, on a night he would never forget, he met and fell in love with Darla Clark. He used to tell his buds that Darla was his ebony princess, and the fact that she had married him was right out of a fairy tale. "Beauty and the Beast," he'd say. Darla was everything that he was not—poised, articulate, and beautiful.

Two years older than Antwone, Darla Clark had graduated from San Diego State and was in her second year as a fifth-grade teacher. For the first time in his life, he overcame his natural shyness and courted her aggressively, doubting that they would ever really connect but being compelled by love to try.

Darla told Antwone that she admired his devotion to country and felt he would love her unconditionally, always be faithful, and raise their children with the values and principles he was developing in the Corps. They married just before he shipped out for his second tour in Iraq, this time not as a conquering Marine but as part of a police force, driving around in Humvees and personnel carriers, waiting to be blown up by insurgents.

That's exactly what had happened, and now Darla was here and he would be seeing her for the first time as a cripple. What would he say? What would she say? He didn't know, but he was worried and frightened. For the first time in a long time,

Antwone Carver doubted himself, wondering if his beautiful wife could still find something to love in the young Marine with a body broken by war.

And then—there she was, just as he remembered her, just as he had dreamed of her night after night in the Iraqi desert: the turned-up nose, the full lips, the dark eyes that danced just for him, her hair cut short and stylish, her body tight and toned. She crossed the room, bent over, and kissed him.

"Is it okay?" she asked softly. "To kiss you, I mean?"

He reached up and clasped her to him, nearly lifting her onto the bed. "There's nothing wrong with *this* part of my body," he said, kissing her neck. "It's just my legs."

As he held his wife in their first loving embrace in more than eight months, he sensed that something else might be broken, something that couldn't be fixed, even by love.

chapter three

Brenden loved being a father. He loved it more than anything. Brian and Mora were the lights in his life, and Kat said she could tell. "It's written all over your face," she told him. "You could never tell a lie—your face is too expressive."

"You mean I can't get away with anything?" he joked.

"My dear," she said, "you are an open book, and I can read every page."

RIDING HOME ON THE ferry across the Sound with Nelson at the end of a long day, Brenden was always excited, anticipating the shared time with his family—to balance his life, to chill out, to touch the emotions that made living truly meaningful. He knew he wasn't the only one who felt that way when Nelson's pace picked up as they walked up the ferry's gangway. The big dog loved to be loved, and he got plenty of it from this family.

"You're a lucky dog," Brenden told his friend. "We've come a long way, haven't we, pal? And both of us are getting more than we deserve."

Even while he was working, the dog's tail thumped against the man's leg in a demonstration of pure, unadulterated happiness. Nelson greeted the children the way he always did, as if he had been away on a long journey instead of just at work for the day. He made little crying noises as he licked them, turning in circles and doing cartwheels across the living room from child to child, trying to get every inch of his body patted by the people and then launching off to find a toy, knowing the kids would play with him until everyone was exhausted. And Brenden knew Nelson needed this time to expend more of his high energy.

Observing the activity, Brenden noticed that something was different tonight. Though the game was just as spirited, Brian wasn't playing. Brenden wandered into the kitchen as Kat was preparing dinner. "Something wrong with Brian?" he asked.

Kat placed her knife down on the cutting board and turned to her husband. "I was going to talk to you about it later, but we've had our first incident at school."

"Incident?" Brenden asked. "What happened?"

"Well," Kat said, sighing, "your son felt it was necessary to defend his father's honor."

"Oh?" Brenden queried, his eyebrows rising.

"Yeah," Kat went on. "It seems some kid in his class named Jimmy asked our little man if his dad was blind, and then went on to make fun of you with some kind of 'Blindy, Blindy, Blindy' chant while they were out on the playground."

"So what did Brian do?" Brenden asked.

"He socked him, and then the kid socked him back. So he has his first shiner under his left eye."

"All right!" Brenden said with a hint of a twinkle in his voice. "Did he win the fight?"

"I think so," Kat said. "He just got a black eye. The other kid had a bloody nose and a cut on his lip."

"All right," Brenden said again. "Good job, Brian!"

Kat became more serious. "So, Dr. McCarthy, what do we do about it? I mean, how do we handle this kind of thing?"

Brenden considered it thoughtfully for a moment. "I'm not sure," he admitted. "Remember, I haven't been blind very long. This is all kind of new. Let me start by talking to the little guy when we tuck him into bed."

Kat and Brenden had developed an approach to bedtime that was special and very consistent. After sharing stories together, they alternated the tucking-in responsibilities so they each got to enjoy the last moments before sleep with both children. The condo allowed the children their own bedrooms, and this seemed the best way to keep everyone together but also to provide memorable moments for each parent individually with their son and daughter.

Later, Brenden sat on the end of Brian's bed, rubbing his son's back as he settled down for the night.

"So, Brian," Brenden asked casually, "did you have a little problem at school today?"

The little boy propped himself up on one elbow. "No, Daddy."

"Oh?" Brenden went on. "Your mommy told me you had a fight with one of the kids in your class. Is that true?"

The child answered softly. "Yes."

"Well, Brian," Brenden said, "it's not a good idea to fight unless a guy has a real good reason. Why did you fight with the other boy?"

Brian didn't answer.

"It's okay, Brian," Brenden encouraged, putting an arm around his son and hugging him. "You can tell Daddy. I won't be mad."

"He called you a bad name." Now his son was crying. "He called you a very bad name, Daddy."

"I know," Brenden said. "Your mom told me. He called me 'Blindy,' didn't he?"

"Yes," Brian said. "I hate him, Daddy. I hate him!"

"No, no," Brenden told him quietly. "Sometimes people say some bad things, but they don't really mean it. In fact, a lot of times when people say bad things about another person, it's because they don't know the truth. You know what I think, Brian?" Brenden said, getting an idea. "I think Nelson and I ought to come to school with you and talk to all of the kids about being blind and about the wonderful job Nelson does helping me. What do you think?"

Brian stopped crying and took a big sniff. "That would be good, Daddy," he said. "I think that'd be really good."

"Okay, pal," Brenden said. "I'll call your teacher tomorrow, and we'll fix this. Now, you go to sleep, okay?"

Brian nodded—and soon was dreaming happy thoughts.

A FEW DAYS LATER, Dr. Brenden McCarthy took the morning off. With Nelson on one side and his little boy holding his hand on the other, they entered Brian's first-grade classroom accompanied by the sounds of the kids exclaiming, "Ooh, that's a big dog," and "That's Brian's daddy," and "What's that handle on the dog's back?" and "I'm scared of dogs!"

The teacher was named Mrs. Martin, and she was one of those outstanding educators who always put children first. Having three kids of her own, she understood completely when Brenden called and explained what he wanted to achieve by coming to the classroom. The teacher was excited at the prospect.

"We're very happy to have you, Dr. McCarthy. I'm sure your coming to class will be a wonderful experience for the children."

And so, there they were—Brenden, Brian, and Nelson, who evidently assumed that this whole group of twenty-three children was gathered here just to play with him. Brenden could feel the big dog quivering in his harness, wanting to lick every child he passed, but never breaking his responsibility to the work as they moved to the front of the classroom.

"Children," Mrs. Martin said, "this is Brian's daddy, Dr. Brenden McCarthy, and his guide dog, Nelson. They've come here this morning to share with us so we can learn about what it means to be a blind person."

Brenden put in, "Hi, everybody. As Mrs. Martin said, I am Brian's daddy, and I am blind. Who knows what it means when someone says a person is blind?"

He heard someone raise a hand.

Mrs. Martin called on the little girl in the third row. "Annie, what do you think it means when someone says a person is blind?"

"It means they can't see," the little girl said, sounding slightly embarrassed.

"That's right, Annie," Brenden said. "It means a person can't see. But do you know what?"

"What?" the little girl asked.

"I heard you put your hand up."

"You did?" she said, sounding amazed.

"I sure did. When you lifted your arm, I heard your sleeve make a rustling sound."

"Wow!" the class said together.

"When you're blind," Brenden went on, "you learn to use all of your other senses. Now, who can tell me about the five senses?"

A little boy spoke up. "There's your eyes."

"That's right," Brenden said. "What's your name?"

"Andrew," the boy said.

"And what do you do with your eyes, Andrew?" Brenden asked.

"You see."

"Right. So what other senses do you have?"

A girl in the first row interrupted. "I know, I know!" she said excitedly.

"Good," Brenden told her, "but let's give Andrew a chance first. So what other senses do you have, Andrew?"

"Touch and hearing."

"That's right," Brenden encouraged, "and what else?"

"And smell," Andrew said.

"And what else?" Brenden prompted.

Andrew was stumped, so Brenden turned to the little girl in the front row.

"Okay, let's see if my friend up front here can help. What's your name?"

"Andrea," she said.

"All right, Andrea, what's the fifth sense?"

"Taste," Andrea said proudly.

"That's right," Brenden told them all. "So there's sight and hearing and smell and taste and . . . What's the last one?" Brenden asked.

"Touch," they said together.

"What are some of your favorite things to touch?" Brenden asked.

Now the children responded eagerly.

"My dog's fur," one said.

"My cat," another put in.

"A flower," a little girl added.

"My daddy's head," a boy in the back row chimed in.

Brenden chuckled. "Why your daddy's head?" he asked.

"Because it's bald," the little boy said, "and it's so smooth."

Everybody laughed.

Brenden took the class through all five senses, getting some great responses and loving the whole experience. He had brought several things with him, including a Braille book and a slate and stylus to show the children how he could read and write.

Actually, he admitted to himself, *I'm not very good at Braille. I only use it occasionally, but I can fake it enough here.*

He then showed the kids the cane he used for mobility before Nelson came into his life. As always, holding the white stick in his hand brought back difficult memories of his early days of blindness, and he was glad to move on, demonstrating for the children his talking alarm clock and his voice-actuated laptop computer.

Before talking about Nelson, he asked if any of the children had questions.

A little girl asked, "Do you have dreams?"

"I sure do," Brenden told her.

"Well, can you see things in your dreams? I mean, are you blind when you dream?"

"That is a very good question," Brenden said. "Yes, blind people are blind when they dream, and in their dreams people talk a lot. It's like turning on the radio instead of a television. In these dreams, people talk and talk and talk and talk."

Everyone laughed.

"Can you see color?" a little boy wanted to know.

"No," Brenden said. "Remember, my eyes are broken."

"But when *I* shut *my* eyes," the little boy went on, "I can see black."

"That's right," Brenden told him. "That's because your brain is still trying to help your eyes see."

That caused everybody to think for a minute.

"How do you know if people are pretty or not?" a little girl asked.

"Everyone's pretty as far as I'm concerned," Brenden told them. "I think people are beautiful. And the wonderful thing is no two people are exactly the same. What makes them special is that they're all different. All of us are special because there's no one else like us."

A boy asked, "Do you think black people are beautiful?"

"Absolutely," Brenden said. "I think black people are really beautiful, and white people are beautiful."

"How about Japanese people?" a little girl said.

"Japanese people are beautiful," Brenden said enthusiastically. "All kinds of people. Everyone is special. Everyone is different. Everyone is beautiful."

The class clapped their hands.

"I think your doggy is beautiful," a little girl said.

"Oh, he is," Brenden said. "Nelson is one of the smartest creatures in the world, too, and he has a very special job."

Brian jumped in to help. "He's a guide dog," Brian proudly told his classmates. "Nelson helps my daddy go to work every day and ride the ferry, and they go jogging together in the morning, and sometimes he takes my dad on trips all by themselves."

A little girl asked, "Does your dog always wear that thing on his back?"

Brenden laughed. "You mean his harness? Oh no," he said. "When Nelson's harness is on, that means he's working. It's like wearing a uniform. But when I take it off, and we're at home, he's Brian's best friend, and he's just a dog like any other dog. It's kind of like when you go to school. You work hard when you're in the classroom, and then when you go home, you get to play. Nelson loves to play."

In response to his master's voice, the big dog thumped his tail on the floor, making all the children laugh.

Brenden stood up, and so did the dog.

"Outside, Nelson. Let's go. Find the door, boy!" The black Lab moved easily through the crowd of kids and put his nose right on the doorknob of the classroom.

This got another "wow" from the children.

"That's awesome," a little boy said.

"What's your name?" Brenden asked.

"I'm Jimmy," the boy said.

And Brenden remembered. "Come here, Jimmy. Let me let *you* feel how Nelson does his job."

The little boy walked up to Nelson and took the harness in his left hand.

"Brian, would you come here and help me, please? Okay, Jimmy," Brenden said, "now Brian's going to take me back to my chair, and Nelson will follow us, so you'll feel how he guides you."

The teacher smiled, knowing exactly what was happening.

"Okay, Brian," Brenden said, "show me where my chair is."

Brian guided his dad expertly back to his chair, and Nelson obediently followed, with Jimmy feeling the pressure in the harness.

"Whoa, cool! It's like . . . It's like water-skiing," Jimmy said, laughing. "He almost pulled me off my feet."

"Well," Brenden said, "I'm a big guy, so he has to pull pretty hard to drag me around."

Brenden went on with his explanation. "Nelson knows a lot of different words—*inside*, *outside*, *find the chair*. He knows escalators and elevators. He knows how to stop at curbs when I'm going to cross a street and how to watch the traffic to make sure we're safe and won't get hit by any cars."

"He's a wonder dog!" a little girl exclaimed.

"Yes, he is," Brenden agreed, "but he's also my best friend, and that's something everyone needs—a best friend. It's easy to have good friends," Brenden told them, "when you take time to learn about the other person and how they feel. Today you've learned about what it means to be blind, so it'll be easier for you to have a blind friend the next time you meet one."

LATER THAT NIGHT, AS Brenden tucked Brian in, the little boy said, "After you left school today, Daddy, Jimmy asked me if I would like to come to his house and play."

"That's great," Brenden said. "That's exactly what I hoped would happen."

"I love you, Daddy," the boy said, hugging his father.

"I love you, too, my little man. Thanks for sticking up for me."

"It's okay, Dad," the boy said, sounding like an adult.

chapter four

"Dr. Blinky, I presume." The voice boomed through the line, forcing Brenden to quickly pull the phone away from his ear.

"Bad News Barnes! To what do I owe the honor of this conversation?"

"It's simple, my boy; you're blessed because I'm going to be coming to your fair city for an American Legion convention—you know, those of us heroes who have fought for our country. I expect you to pay homage to my service with a dinner cooked by the beautiful Kathleen, in your island paradise, with enough time to play with the children, drink expensive scotch—at least twelve-year-old Macallan—and smoke cigars out on your deck, of course. Preferably Cubans, if you can find some."

Brenden opened his mouth to reply, but his friend's bombast

continued. "I'm sure none of this will be an imposition, as you owe me big time for making you the successful psychiatrist you are today, living the good life and charging patients exorbitant hourly fees for your service, fees that those of us who are simply humble counselors never receive for the work we do."

"You don't need compensation," Brenden said, laughing, "because you're a crusader for the rights of those less fortunate. At least that's what you always told me when you were lifting me out of my own depression."

"True, true, my boy," Barnes agreed, "but I have expensive and exquisite tastes. It's a weakness in my character. So prepare the dinner, bring the scotch, and don't forget the cigars. I'll be joining you in a week."

"Bad News," Brenden said to his friend, "that's the best news I've heard in a long, long time. See you soon, pal."

McCarthy hung up and sat back in his chair with a large smile creasing his face. Dr. Marvin "Bad News" Barnes, former first-round NFL draft pick and a Vietnam veteran who had been blinded in combat, was the person responsible for jarring Brenden into living again. Barnes was Brenden's intake counselor at the Colorado Rehabilitation Center for the Blind, and his no-nonsense approach, administered with intelligence and an uncompromising attitude, provided Brenden with the kick in the pants that made possible the life he now so very much enjoyed.

Brenden loved the giant of a man with the enormous personality. The bond they shared had gone far beyond counselor and patient. They were family.

KAT WENT ALL OUT for the dinner with their friend. A cheese platter and some wonderful Greek spanakopita were followed by Washington oysters and a Caesar salad. The main course of prime rib melted on the tongue, along with Kat's famous garlic mashed potatoes and summer squash. Dessert was ice cream and fruit, which delighted the children.

Barnes had only met Brenden's children once before, and though Mora had taken to him immediately, Brian considered him a giant and was a little shy around him. The shyness evaporated when the big man produced a football autographed by the entire Denver Broncos team and a promise that if Brenden and Brian could get to Colorado, Barnes would procure sideline passes from Coach Mike Shanahan to make the game up close and personal for the little boy.

Barnes's infectious personality and boisterous humor charmed the whole family, and by the end of dinner, when the men moved outside to enjoy their cigars, everyone was feeling full and terrific.

Surrounded by the rich smell of Havana tobacco, Brenden asked, "So what goes on at these American Legion conferences, Marvin, besides the swapping of old war stories?"

"A lot," Barnes said. "Remember, we're a nation at war, and veterans are paying a horrible price. There are over five thousand dead and well over forty thousand men and women wounded, man! Most of the American people have forgotten the war in Afghanistan, and Iraq—well, Iraq is Iraq. None of our guys feel good about it because they don't feel that they're winning. Unlike the war in Vietnam, the public is mostly sympathetic toward the vets, but these fellows come home wondering if their sacrifice has been truly relevant."

"I hear that," Brenden said.

"Then there's the question of the conditions. You've probably read about the problems at VA hospitals like Walter Reed. When a federal bureaucracy runs the show and there is no competition, maintenance and care seem to fall to the basement. Plus, there's the added problem of patient compensation. There are thousands of guys waiting months, even years, for their cases to be effectively reviewed in order to determine how much they should be receiving per month. We have countless wounded veterans who are receiving only a minimal subsidy because the system is so inefficient."

"I've read a little about that. Seems so unjust," Brenden said.

"I'll tell you something, Brenden; what's most unjust—more than anything else—is that these men feel betrayed by our military and our government. So many of them feel alone and helpless. I spend a lot of my time counseling them, at least the ones in Colorado I can see, and I feel fairly effective because they think of me as one of them. But more than that, they accept the idea that, as a disabled person, I'm talking to them from a point of real understanding. That makes them believe I'm personally engaged."

As in years past, the big man dropped a huge arm over Brenden's shoulders and gave him a fatherly squeeze. "You know, Dr. McCarthy, you could make a big difference in the lives of some of these vets if you wanted to get involved."

Having tucked the children into bed, Kat joined the men on

the deck, not saying anything about the cigar smoke. "What should Brenden be involved in?" she asked, coming in on the last part of the conversation.

Brenden moved to a chair and sat, knowing his wife's question would continue the uncomfortable dialogue.

"Counseling disabled vets," Barnes said, turning to Kat. "Brenden's clinical background and his personal experience make him someone I know they'd listen to, particularly, as so many of them are facing PTSD . . ."

"You mean post-traumatic stress disorder?" Kat asked.

"That's right," Barnes said. "It's part of all wars, but when you come home feeling irrelevant, the trauma seems to be exacerbated."

"I've read about some of the studies in my journals," Brenden said. "There are some new drug protocols that seem to be helping veterans, but I suppose if it's not addressed, it can become an epidemic, ruining many lives."

Barnes was intense. "It can ruin families, man, shatter marriages, destroy self-worth, and, frankly, make it seem like life is not worth living."

"It sounds horrible," Kat said. "I mean, that the system is failing these guys, and that they feel abandoned by their own country."

"That's not quite true," Barnes said. "The American public is sympathetic. It's the bureaucrats and the professionals who aren't getting the job done."

Brenden found himself tensing. He could sense where this conversation was going.

Barnes plowed ahead. "The patient load is far too great for the system to handle, and the VA is looking for doctors who will work cases pro bono."

"Pro bono," Brenden echoed. *For the common good.*

"That's right, my boy. Pro bono," Barnes said. "And I think you'd be perfect for the job."

Brenden felt sweat dripping onto his shirt, even though the night was cool. "I don't know, Marvin," he said. "I'm at the stage where my practice is growing rapidly, and I already have a patient load that's taking most of my time. I just don't know if I can help."

"You mean you don't know *if* you will help," the big man said, his tone changing, expressing disappointment.

"Listen, Marvin," Brenden said, trying to explain, "the truth is, I'm not sure that I've had enough time adjusting to my own disability."

"How much time is enough?" Barnes asked. "How many more years do you need?"

"You're probably right," Brenden agreed, "but I just don't know if I'm able—or ready—to do something like that. Not yet."

Barnes reached into his pocket and took out a card, passing it to Brenden. "Well, here's the number for the VA hospital here in Seattle, along with the name of the administrator of the psych section. I've already spoken to him and sold him on the idea that you'd be great at the job."

The big man took a long pull on his cigar and spoke pointedly. "Brenden, you can't fight for your country because you went blind, but you can serve your nation by making a difference in the lives of some of these young men."

Brenden wanted to speak. He wanted to fight back. He wanted to argue with his friend, but the impact of the man's words made him close his mouth.

Kat broke the tension, offering brandy and chocolate-dipped strawberries. Barnes graciously dropped the subject, allowing the evening to become light once again; yet to all of them the next forty-five minutes seemed tense, the joking awkward, the frivolity artificial.

Brenden was thankful that the hour was late and it was time for bed. So with Barnes settled in the guest room downstairs, Brenden and Kat quietly headed up to their room.

As they went through their nighttime routines, neither wanted to broach the subject of Barnes's conversation. Kat was thinking that there were issues in her husband's adjustment to blindness that were too complicated for her to ever understand, and Brenden was wondering if once again his friend had been testing his character by suggesting that he get involved professionally in the needs of war-ravaged vets.

In a way, he was angry at Barnes for imposing the idea of service on him. Wasn't he already doing enough to make a difference in the lives of others? Did he have to take on the complexity in the psyches of these disabled men? He knew Barnes believed that you would never be whole again until you found a way to give back to the disabled community, but oddly, Brenden believed that he was not one of *them*—the handicapped, the disabled. Even though his eyes were broken, Brenden still felt like the young man who had later returned with Nelson to the mountain that had taken his sight and conquered it, putting his disability aside and breaking its hold on him.

Is every person with a disability obligated to get involved? he wondered.

In the dark, unable to sleep, he asked Kat, "So what do you think? Is Marvin right? Do I have a responsibility to get involved with these vets?"

"I don't know, honey. What do you think?" his wife asked.

Brenden hated when she put the question right back on him like that. "I don't know, Kat. I mean, I'm trying to help the patients I already have. Why would I be obligated to do pro bono work with disabled vets?"

"Because right now," she said candidly, "at this point in time, those are the people who could benefit the most from your"—she paused, looking for the words—"your personal expertise."

He recoiled at her words, and she touched his cheek. "That's not . . . Brenden, that's not what I mean. The truth is, Barnes is right. Those guys will believe that you understand because, though you didn't lose your sight during military service, the accident—your loss—was just as traumatic."

"But, Kat," he said, "I haven't been to war. I don't understand it."

"But you can learn," she said, "by asking questions, by being empathetic, by using your skills as a doctor and your talent as a therapist to put yourself in their place. And most importantly, you can use your goodness as a person." She paused for a moment then asked gently, "Brenden, do you know why I love you?"

"Because I'm handsome," he joked.

"Because you're human," she told him in the dark. "Because you are the most human person I know, and it's in the blending of your humanity, your particular understanding, and your professional skills that you can really make a difference. So I believe you have to. Look, call this administrator up at the VA, try one case, and see how you feel. If you don't connect, at least you gave it a shot. I don't think Marvin will hold you responsible for more than that."

"Okay," Brenden said, sighing. "Let me sleep on that. I'll talk to Marvin in the morning."

Kat snuggled next to her husband, her back fitting perfectly against him in that intimate way reserved for people who are in love.

"You'll figure it out, Brenden. You'll get it right. I love you."

He kissed her neck, and in minutes they were asleep.

THE NEXT MORNING, THEY had a simple breakfast of coffee, juice, and blueberry muffins. And Nelson was forced to take on a new challenge.

Since it was Saturday, Brenden would not be going in to work, but he insisted on getting Marvin settled on the ferryboat, with Kat staying home to watch the children. This would require Nelson to guide not only his blind master but also the blind giant who would be holding Brenden's other arm.

"You really think we can do this?" Barnes asked.

"Absolutely," Brenden said, "as long as you don't trip. I'm sure Nelson will provide enough space—if there is enough space to accommodate your big butt," he joked. "You'll get through just fine."

They went down in the elevator and crossed to the departure dock; it was much easier than Brenden's trip a week earlier with his cane.

"Who is the captain today?" Brenden asked the ticket taker as he prepared to board.

"Captain Johns," the man said.

Brenden had come to know most of the crew during the time they had lived on the island, and Eric Johns was a young and enthusiastic seaman.

Introducing them, Brenden asked the captain if he would make sure Barnes got a cab to his conference when they docked in Seattle.

"No problem," the captain said. "There'll be plenty of cabs hanging around on a weekend."

Brenden hugged his friend.

"Look, Marvin," he said, "I don't know if I'll be any good working with veterans, but I promise I'll call the hospital administrator and take on at least one pro bono case."

The return hug nearly crushed Brenden's ribs. "That's my boy," the giant said. "I knew you would come around. Call me if you have any problems or if I can be of any help."

"Oh, you'll hear from me," Brenden said. "This is all your

fault. I know I'm in way over my head, and I'll need all the advice you can give me."

"This was a great visit," Barnes said. "Thank Kat for me, and tell her there'll be dinner at our house next winter when you guys come skiing."

"Sounds good," McCarthy said. "I'll expect a bottle of Midleton Irish waiting for me when I show up."

"And you'll have it, young doctor. Even on my limited resources."

The men hugged again, and Brenden said good-bye to his friend, surprising Nelson with the change from his weekday routine—instead of boarding the ferry, he cued the dog to retreat back down the gangway and head home for a quiet Saturday with the family.

chapter five

Dr. Jonathan Craig placed the chart neatly on his desk and studied his hands. He loved his hands. They were long and strong, the nails perfectly groomed; they were the hands of one of those hand models in commercials or a great pianist, or, in his case, the hands of one of the most respected neurosurgeons in the country.

One day a week he gave his time to the military here at Seattle Veterans Hospital. From his office window on the top floor of the administration building on the top of Beacon Hill, he could look out over the bay and then let his eyes take in the mountain vistas to the west. All in all, it was a wonderful setting, and he thought of his time here as doing something important for his country—even though by anyone else's standards he was well compensated for his work.

Others sometimes called him arrogant, but he supposed there was a major difference between arrogance and confidence. He liked to think—though his two ex-wives would disagree—that he was supremely and appropriately confident. He was an Ivy League man all the way. He had attended Yale as an undergraduate and then Harvard Medical School, where he had graduated in the top ten of his class. After residency he had migrated to the Northwest, believing that his talent was needed in what he thought of as the hinterlands of America, and he had been right.

Big bucks followed. Though he was paying two alimonies, his lucrative real estate investments, along with timely positions in the stock market, had made him a wealthy man. For him, wealth meant that if he retired tomorrow at forty-five, he could continue his lifestyle unchanged, living on the interest from his capital investments.

The chart he had just reviewed was on Corporal Antwone Carver. He sighed, understanding that even with his talent, the Marine's prognosis was not good. He noted that Carver had a complete transection of the spinal cord, meaning total separation at—he looked down again at the chart—at thoracic or T-10. Turning in his chair, he studied the skeletal model on his wall and sighed again, thinking about how he would explain the devastating condition to the young man.

He rehearsed it in his mind. If you drew a line across a person's navel, below that line would be a loss of all reflex. He decided he would show the Marine what he meant by doing a couple of tests. Show-and-tell was always a better method in these cases. It left no room for doubt. He would begin with the pinprick test and then follow it up with the traditional tuning fork demonstration, in which the fork does not vibrate because there is no stimulus response from the muscle. Even by expanding the tuning fork test to the old ping hammer test on the knee, there would be no reflex. Ergo, the man would have to face the reality of his condition without developing any false hope. Dr. Jonathan Craig believed very much in leaving no doubt—absolutely no doubt—in the mind of a patient.

It doesn't do them any good to give them hope, he thought. *If I can't fix them, why should I lie to them?* This was especially true in cases like Carver's, because often, after a few days, patients became hyperreflexive. The muscles, spasming, could easily give the impression that feeling was coming back and that they would one day walk again.

Dr. Craig knew there were great possibilities for spinal injury patients with the development of genetic mapping and electronic stimulation, but the probability was that spinal cord injuries of this kind would not be corrected surgically during Carver's lifetime. Given that set of parameters, honesty is always the best policy, as his mother used to say.

He noted that Carver was retaining a great deal of urine in his bladder, indicating that he was losing tone and was becoming flaccid in the anal sphincter. A catheter that would likely be permanent would drain the urine, but the man would have to face a lifetime of colon cleaning by an ongoing series of embarrassing enemas—not pleasant but livable, and certainly better than having to be bagged. Not that Dr. Craig needed any more support for his prognosis, but he also saw that the chart indicated positive Babinski. This is when the toes involuntarily point upward, almost as if the patient was stiffening in the throes of death.

He decided that the doctors in country had done the right stuff. A complete spinal X-ray and MRI had been taken, supporting the diagnosis. They had treated Carver with large doses of corticosteroids in an effort to bring down the swelling. With the swelling reduced, there was nothing left to doubt in the prognosis. Corporal Antwone Carver was now a paraplegic. Craig was sure of that fact as he put on his blazer, straightened his tie, and prepared to visit the patient.

Just tell it to him straight, he told himself. *Better to get it over with and let the kid begin to deal with it.*

Doing the obligatory knock and then entering the room, he saw that Carver was not alone. A beautiful woman was sitting with him and holding his hand; Dr. Craig assumed she must be his wife.

Darn, he thought. *That means there'll be tears. I hate it when the spouses are here. It complicates the conversation, especially when you have to talk about sexual function. Well, let's get it done.*

Dr. Craig cleared his throat. "Corporal Carver?" he said, crossing to the bedside. "I'm Dr. Jonathan Craig, the neurosurgeon reviewing your case."

"Thank you, Doctor," the man said from the bed as the woman stood and put out her hand. The surgeon noted that she was strikingly beautiful, even exotic. He loved exotic women. He always had. And this one was a stunner. She wore very little makeup. Her high cheekbones and dark eyes seemed in perfect balance with her full lips and great body. Her toned legs caused him to struggle to concentrate.

"I'm Antwone's wife, Darla," she said, interrupting his wandering thoughts. "We are both very grateful for your help, Dr. Craig. Do you have recommendations for a course of treatment?"

Not only gorgeous but well spoken and intelligent, he thought. *What a shame she'll be denied a lifetime of sexual pleasure.*

Again the doctor cleared his throat. "Yes, well, about the case . . ."

As before, the woman held the man's hand, and both sets of eyes were on the doctor's face.

"Before I talk about your prognosis, let me show you some things."

Over the next few minutes, Dr. Craig went through the song and dance of pinprick, tuning fork, and ping hammer, demonstrating the lack of feeling or reflex from the waist down. He observed that the woman remained extremely composed and that the man seemed to be handling it all with stoic bravery.

Good for them, Craig mused. *Nice to see people who are courageous, rather than whiny or overdramatic.*

At the end of the show-and-tell, the doctor put down his demonstration tools. "So you see," he said, looking directly at the young Marine, "it is clear that you have no feeling from the abdomen down. You have suffered a complete severing of the spinal cord, bringing about your present paralysis."

The man in the bed turned his head away and buried his face

in the pillow, not looking at Dr. Craig. But the woman's eyes never left the doctor's face. It was she who spoke.

"Okay," she said, "Antwone's paralyzed. I've been reading a lot about guys in chairs and how much they've done with their lives." She reached out and touched her husband's face. "Antwone? Antwone, look at me, please. We can handle this together. I know we can. I love you, Antwone."

The doctor dropped his eyes, feeling embarrassed as the woman leaned over and kissed her husband. *Embarrassed? Is that what I'm feeling?* Craig wondered. *Or is it something else? Jealousy? No, no, I'd call it envy.* Nodding to himself, he knew those thoughts were for another time, and he pushed them out of his head for the moment, going on with his discourse.

"There is another issue that needs to be discussed," the doctor stated.

Both young people turned to him, their eyes questioning.

"Other issues?" It was the woman who spoke.

"Yes, ma'am." Dr. Craig paused, looking directly at Darla as he spoke. "I mean that along with total paralysis from the waist down, there is also the loss of sexual function."

The room was silent for a moment, and then a sound came from the man in the bed; it began as a low, soft "no" and crescendoed to a guttural sound that became a high-pitched wail that sent a chill down the doctor's back. "Noooooooooo!"

The woman was holding her husband now, rocking him gently, talking quietly, and soothing him. "It's okay, baby. It's okay," she was saying. "It's okay. I love you, baby. I love you. It's okay."

Dr. Craig rose, wanting to avoid this tableau of wasted emotions. Sure, it wasn't easy for a man to accept impotence, but what choice did he have? The Marine was still alive, wasn't he? He had made it through the war, hadn't he? And he had come home to this strong, beautiful woman.

Craig cleared his throat, interrupting the couple's intimate moment. "I'll be consulting with your physical therapist and your occupational therapist about their recommendations for a course of treatment. In the meantime, I'll prescribe some medication to help you sleep and recommend a psychiatric consult."

The man's keening had now become a more controlled moaning, and the woman was clearly in charge of the situation. "Thank you, Dr. Craig," she said.

Craig reached into his wallet and pulled out a beautifully embossed business card. Removing a pen from his jacket, he wrote his cell number on the back.

"Feel free to call me anytime," he said, handing it to the woman. His fingers lingered a moment on hers, and he gave her the warm smile that always worked on the women he hit on. "Please let me know if there's anything I can do to make your husband more comfortable or"—he gently let go of her hand, his fingers subtly brushing her bare leg—"if I can help you in any way." He looked at her meaningfully, making sure she caught his insinuation.

The woman quickly pulled her hand away. "Thank you, Doctor," she said coolly. "We'll call if we need anything." Immediately she turned back to her husband.

I've been dismissed! I can't believe it, Dr. Craig thought. *Okay then, good luck, little girlie. Have a good life.*

With dignity in his step and his ego firmly in place, the doctor strolled out of the room and closed the door. Looking at his watch, he decided that even though it was early in the afternoon, he'd had quite enough of needless emotional engagement for one day. *I think I'll go to the club, play a little squash, have a massage, and then treat myself to a couple of martinis and a fine dinner. I'm not operating for a couple of days, so there's time for some of the good life.*

As he walked down the hall and took the elevator to the parking garage, he shook his head twice, putting Antwone Carver and his beautiful wife, not just on the back burner of his mind, but right out of his head.

BRENDEN KEPT HIS PROMISE to his friend and called Dr. William Harrison, the director of the psychiatric department at Seattle Veterans Hospital, located high above the city at the top of Beacon Hill. Harrison agreed to meet McCarthy for lunch in the hospital's cafeteria on Tuesday afternoon and then follow it up with a tour so that Brenden could get a feel for the facility.

As Brenden tended to do, he forgot to tell the unsuspecting Dr. Harrison that he was blind, so it came as quite a shock to the gray-haired psychiatrist when the tall, blond, blind doctor arrived for lunch with a big black Lab named Nelson as a third party. It was obvious to Brenden right away that Dr. Harrison was not an animal person.

"You mean the dog makes rounds with you, Dr. McCarthy? He's involved in your daily patient caseload?"

"Sure!"

"Isn't that somewhat disconcerting?" Dr. Harrison asked. "Some people are not . . . I mean, not everyone has a predisposition to like dogs."

Brenden had heard this kind of thing before, so his response came easily. "It's been interesting, Dr. Harrison. I think of Nelson as a therapy dog, and in that role he brings almost all of my patients a terrific sense of comfort, even those who might be somewhat frightened at first. I find that after they spend some time with him, they tend to overcome their fear—and that in itself, I believe, is healthy."

As he spoke, he reached down and stroked Nelson's fur, reassuring both the dog and himself. He made a mental note: *I'll bet this guy will never get comfortable with Nelson.*

Brenden also noticed that Harrison had an annoying habit of constantly playing with his pen, clicking it repeatedly, suggesting that his mind was elsewhere or that he was nervous and overwhelmed by his responsibilities.

After ordering their food—a chicken sandwich and soup for Harrison and a tuna on sourdough for Brenden—Harrison finally stopped flicking his pen and leaned in close to Brenden. "I was delighted to get your call, Dr. McCarthy. Frankly, we're completely overloaded here. We really don't have time for one-on-one patient engagement. Almost everything we do is group based because we're so understaffed, due to federal cutbacks."

"Cutbacks?" Brenden queried. "In the middle of a war?"

The doctor sighed. "Sadly, it's much easier to procure money to carry on the killing than it is to provide funding for healing. There's been no retrofitting for veterans hospitals around the country for the last twenty years. Even with all the hubbub over conditions at Walter Reed, there hasn't been any trickle-down effect that I've noticed."

Dr. Harrison was back to flicking his pen again, only now Brenden understood that the nervous quirk was based on real frustration.

"Anyway, Dr. McCarthy, you're going to be working with Corporal Antwone Carver, an African-American Marine from Compton who has suffered complete spinal cord separation and paralysis from the waist down."

Dr. Harrison sighed. "His case has been reviewed by our best neurosurgeon, Dr. Jonathan Craig, confirming the in-country diagnosis. From my visit with Corporal Carver, beyond the expected deep depression, I think you can assume the onset of post-traumatic stress disorder."

"Certainly," Brenden agreed. "It's highly likely. It'll be at the top of my list when evaluating him."

"I'm glad you're with us, Dr. McCarthy. Let me show you and your friend to your temporary office space, and then we'll take a walk around the ward to give you a feeling for our overworked facility."

WHAT STRUCK BRENDEN MOST on his tour was the quiet in the place. It was as if the patients had drawn inside themselves, and when he spoke to them, asking them how they were, almost all of them gave the same answer.

"I'm fine," they would say, or "No problem, Doc."

When he asked if they were being well cared for, the answer was similar, something like, "I guess people are doing the best they can," or "All I really want to do is get out of here."

Brenden wasn't a fool. He didn't expect a veterans hospital to be a festive place, but what worried him was the pall of sadness and apathy that hung like the Seattle fog in every corner of the hospital.

At the end of the hour, he, Nelson, and Dr. Harrison were back in the cramped office Brenden would be using. Nelson sprawled under the desk as if he understood that they would be doing some work in the crowded space.

"I'll inform Dr. Craig that you'll be taking on Antwone Carver's case," Dr. Harrison said.

"Fine," Brenden said, handing him a card. "There's my office, answering service, and e-mail. Please tell him I'd be happy to talk with him at his convenience."

"Okay," Harrison said, shaking hands. "We're glad to have you on the team. Good luck with your first case, Dr. McCarthy."

"Thank you," Brenden said. "I'll do the best I can."

When Harrison was gone, Brenden sat in the squeaky chair with Nelson at his feet, considering how much he had to learn about the issues confronting veterans of war. As he often did when challenged by the problems of a new patient, he found himself reaching down and patting the big dog. There was so much comfort in touching the animal. To Brenden, it was as if bonding with Nelson reassured him that he could connect with Antwone Carver.

He hoped that was true.

chapter six

Brenden couldn't believe it. He had just received a cursory e-mail from Dr. Jonathan Craig, and its contents revealed all he needed to know about where this guy was coming from.

To: *Dr. Brenden McCarthy*
From: *Dr. Jonathan Craig*
Subject: *Patient Antwone Carver*

Corporal Carver has suffered complete separation of the spinal cord. Paralysis is permanent, including sexual function. The patient is depressed and unresponsive. Please consult.

What was it about surgeons that made them so arrogant and dysfunctional when it came to expressing any semblance of empathy and appropriate postoperative patient care? Brenden sat back in his chair, wondering—not for the first time—why people like Dr. Craig even enter the medical profession. Sadly, he agreed with many of his friends who believed that being a surgeon—most particularly, a surgeon with a significant subspecialty—caused them to become isolated in their technical skills, prompting them to lose their connection with patients.

Actually, looking at it with his clinical eye rather than his personal bias, Brenden reasoned that doctors like Craig were like Olympic athletes going for the gold. Their myopic view focused on one objective and on one person: themselves. Then when they failed somewhere in life, as everyone does, they fell back on their basic survival tactic: avoidance. They blocked their lack of achievement from their minds as they focused on their personal goals once again.

Brenden's education in orthopedic surgery came to mind. If he had completed his residency, what type of surgeon would he have become? He was an entirely different person now—not just because he had adapted to blindness successfully, but because he had changed on the inside. His focus had moved outward, away from himself, and, ironically, he was happier as a result.

To be fair, Brenden had met some extraordinary surgeons, but he had come to think of these colleagues as the mechanics of medicine. It was the diagnosticians who demonstrated they cared and were the true healers. Both his personal and professional experience had solidified this belief.

"Okay," he sighed, muttering out loud to Nelson, who was resting at his feet. "Let's get to the case of Antwone Carver."

Brenden rose, straightened his tie, and put on his sports jacket. As he did, Nelson shook himself and moved to the heel position, so that when his master dropped his left hand, it fell naturally over the handle of the harness.

"You're always ready, aren't you, boy?" Brenden grabbed hold of the harness. "I sure hope I am." Man and dog headed to the fifth floor and their meeting with Antwone Carver.

As they moved down the hall to the elevator, Brenden mentally reviewed the patient's intake notes. Antwone Carver had been injured when an IED blew up the personnel carrier he was riding in, killing the other three Marines and leaving Carver paralyzed. He noted that Carver was married and had grown up in Los Angeles. The profile also indicated that he was an African-American with a high-school education.

Not much to go on, Brenden thought. *I really will be flying blind on this one.*

Brenden had developed a technique that seemed to work well when he was introduced to a new patient in a hospital setting. He would allow the nurse to precede him into the room, putting Nelson on the follow command. This would bring them to the side of the bed—or in this case, to the patient's wheelchair—allowing him to put out his hand for the initial awkward handshake. He knew that his blindness often made patients uncomfortable, so for a while he had considered not making Nelson part of the first meeting, but he had discovered that it was better for the patients to deal with his blindness up front than wonder about it as their clinical relationship developed.

One thing was for sure: when he came into the room accompanied by the big black dog with a harness on his back, their entrance was not missed by Corporal Antwone Carver.

"Corporal Carver," the nurse said by way of introduction, "this is Dr. Brenden McCarthy. He'd like to speak with you for a few minutes, if you don't mind."

Brenden put his hand out and waited, with it suspended in air, for the usual clasp, but it didn't come. McCarthy heard the Marine push himself backward in his wheelchair until it bumped the wall.

He tried to bridge the gap verbally.

"Hi, Antwone. I'm Dr. Brenden McCarthy," he said. "Dr. Craig suggested I come and spend some time with you, see if there's anything I might be able to do to be helpful."

No response came from Carver, so Brenden went on.

"This is my friend Nelson. Would you like to meet him?"

That got a response.

"That's a big dog," the man said warily. "A real big dog."

"Yes, he is," Brenden said, "but he's quite special, you know. He's a guide dog."

"Don't matter," Carver said. "He can bite you just like any other."

"Not Nelson." Brenden laughed easily. "He might lick you to death, but he'd never bite. Anyway, let me pull up a chair, and I'll tie him to it so that he won't be able to intrude on our conversation. Is that okay with you?"

"Okay," he said, not really meaning it.

"Will that be all, Doctor?" the nurse put in.

"Yes, thank you, Amy. That'll be all for now."

Her shoes squeaked their way out of the room, and Brenden settled himself into the armchair she had pulled up for him, sitting directly across from Carver.

After tying Nelson to the chair, Dr. McCarthy leaned back, crossed his legs, and rested his arms on the chair, remembering that Kat had told him this position looked very conversational.

Immediately he noticed that Carver was fidgeting. He heard the man's fingers drumming on the arms of his wheelchair. He heard the swishing sound of Carver's head swiveling from side to side, as if he was searching for something. He kept making some kind of clicking sound in his mouth. And when he spoke, his words were almost unintelligible because the speech pattern was so quick. His autonomic nervous system was going wild.

Brenden noted all the signs of post-traumatic stress disorder—a postwar disorder that was shattering untold numbers of lives.

The doctor tried to create some form of simpatico.

"So, Antwone . . . May I call you Antwone? Corporal Carver sounds a little formal, don't you think?"

Again no response, so the psychiatrist went on.

"Antwone, you're from LA, huh?"

Still no response.

"Your intake says that you were raised in Compton. Pretty tough neighborhood, I'm thinking."

Still nothing from Carver.

"Your Marine Corps bio says that this was your second tour. For hobbies, it lists music and basketball. Are you a Lakers fan?"

That at least got the man to nod his head. Brenden heard the movement and was encouraged.

"Me, too, although I've never understood how they could have traded Shaq."

Still no direct engagement, so Brenden kept working.

"But you know what?" he said. "This kid, Andrew Bynum, really might be something, and they're getting great backcourt play from Jordan Farmar, the kid out of UCLA. What do you think about their bringing Derek Fisher back? Do you think it was a good move?"

"The man can play."

Ah, Brenden thought, *a mini breakthrough.*

"Yes, he can," Brenden agreed. "He can really ball, but more than that, I think he's an important psychological balance for Kobe because they played together in three championships. Did you play the game a lot growing up, Antwone?"

Brenden was surprised when he got an answer.

"All the time, man. I was king of the court. I had the sweetest jump shot you ever saw. Would've made it in the pros, too, even though I'm small. There've been a lot of small guys that have made it—Spud Webb, Tiny Archibald, Calvin Murphy, and now Steve Nash and Chris Paul. I was as good as any of them. I know it."

"It's good when you know something," Brenden suggested.

"We all need to know we're good at something. Listen, if you don't mind, I need to ask you some questions. I know they'll seem a little boring, but you know how it is. There's always paperwork to fill out; the military marches down the road of red tape."

Back to no response.

Brenden had seen this kind of behavior with civilians before, but for some reason, in the case of veterans, the depression seemed to be extraordinarily complex and profound. He had learned from Dr. Williams that hospital rules required the chart to be filled out in a very specific way, but getting there could often be like pulling teeth. He decided it was time to tell Carver why he was here.

"Listen, Antwone, I probably should have told you I'm a psychiatrist, and Dr. Craig felt that it might be helpful for you and I to spend some time together."

The man's reaction was not untypical. "I don't need to talk to any head doctor," he said. "There's nothing you can do for me."

"Well, maybe that's true," Brenden said. "But just give me a couple of minutes, will you? First of all, can you tell me what happened? I mean, how you got hurt?"

"You already know that from the file," the Marine said. "An IED blew up a personnel carrier I was riding in. Three dead, and I wish I was too."

Too early to push that button, Brenden reminded himself. *Just get the history. Try to create trust.*

"Corporal, have you ever seen a psychologist or psychiatrist before?"

The Marine's laugh was a single note of disgust. "In my neighborhood, man? We just had pimps and pushers, gangs, drug runners, and preachers."

Brenden smiled. "What about the rest of your family? Any of them ever see a professional?"

"Not unless it was in juvie or on the inside."

"You mean prison?" Brenden said. He heard the guy nod. "Okay, I got it. What about chemical dependency?"

The Marine laughed darkly. "You mean drugs? Oh yeah, we got a lot of that in the family. Booze and drugs—I've seen it all."

"How about you, Antwone—any problems with drugs?"

"There would have been," he said. "But the Corps saved me." His voice took on a different sound. "The Corps was my family, man. The Corps was everything."

"I'm sure they still care about you," Brenden said sympathetically. "*Semper fi*. Once a Marine, always a Marine."

"Not when your legs are broke. Not when you can't make it up the hill. Not when you pee through a catheter or have enemas twice a day. Not when you're not a man."

"I don't believe that," Brenden said. "I know I haven't been around here for very long, but from everything I've heard, the Corps cares more than any other military service."

Carver didn't respond, so the doctor went on. "Did you have any illnesses growing up? Any serious stuff?"

"Not until now," the man said. "Not until this."

"What about family support?" Brenden asked. "Has your mother been here to see you? Or . . . let me see, from your records, I see that you're married, right?"

"Yeah," the Marine said, his voice taking on a timbre that sent an alarm through Brenden.

"So has your wife been here to see you?"

"Yeah, she was here," the man said. "But she won't be here for long. Listen," he said, "I've had enough of these questions. You want to get out of my face?"

Brenden pressed just a little. "Antwone, it sounds like you're worried about your relationship with your wife. Is that true?"

Now the man went stone quiet, and Brenden knew that this clearly was the end of the interview.

"Look, Antwone, you're going to be here for a while, and, well, I'd love the chance to talk to you again when you feel more like it."

More silence.

"Okay, I'll see you sometime tomorrow," Brenden told him, not giving the man a choice.

Standing, he forgot he had put the leash around the leg of the chair, and so when Nelson stood, the chair moved.

"Oh, sorry, pal," he said, reaching down and untying the leash. "I forgot you were tied there."

Brenden was always amazed when Nelson took it upon himself to get to know someone. The animal picked certain people to communicate with, and they weren't necessarily the ones who seemed obvious. In this case, the dog moved forward to the end of his leash and sniffed the Marine's hand before Carver could pull it back.

"Get that dog away from me!"

"I'm sorry," Brenden said. "There are just some people he seems to like."

"Get him out of here!" Carver said again. "Take your stupid dog and get out of here!"

Brenden smiled warmly. "Nelson's pretty persistent," he said easily. "He just knows when he likes someone, so I guess we'll have to come back tomorrow."

Turning, the two moved toward the door, and Brenden had the feeling that the Marine's eyes were watching them work, taking it all in but saying nothing.

The doctor turned his head back as they moved outside. "See you tomorrow afternoon, Corporal."

Moving down the hall headed for the elevator, Brenden understood that this was going to be a hard case, and it seemed to him that his first priority was to get the young man to agree to begin a drug protocol. The problem, as always, was that you couldn't impose treatment on a patient; it had to be voluntary. And, as the doctor settled in behind his desk, instinct told him that bringing Antwone Carver to a place where he would accept treatment in any form was going to be difficult.

At the moment, Brenden believed, Carver was a guy who felt that he had nothing to live for.

I remember what that felt like, Brenden thought. *That's exactly what I was feeling when I went blind. Somehow I need to create a level of empathy, and from that maybe I can begin to build some elements of trust. God willing, I'll be able to help.*

Brenden took a cassette machine out of his desk and completed the patient history notes that he would dictate onto Carver's chart. Then, sitting back a little deeper in the chair, he let himself free-associate with the machine still running, trying to clarify his own thinking.

"There are so many layers of life and loss I have to work my way through with Patient Carver, and to do that I need to find touchstones that bring us together. We're men who come from completely different social structures, and if he follows the normal pattern, he probably has an inherent distrust of white people, even though he's worked with many in the Marine Corps. It's clear from our first conversation that the Marines have become his family and that prior to signing up, he did not have a particularly positive self-image. The question of sexuality is going to be the elephant in the room, and that conversation is never easy, especially when there's a wife involved.

"I have the impression that right now it's going to be extremely difficult to find building blocks to restore Carver's mental health. I'll need to get to know his wife, maybe his mother; and maybe there's an aspect of faith in God somewhere in his background we can lean on. I'm going to have to begin very slowly and search carefully for common ground, or I'll lose him. Maybe my own story will create connection. In the end I suppose that's what therapy is really about. You create bonding and trust, and then maybe, as Frankl says, a course of treatment becomes a course of directive action."

Brenden stretched and switched off the cassette.

"What do you think, Nelson?" he said to the big dog. "Do you think it all comes down to trust, with a little love thrown in?"

The dog's tail thumped the floor in complete agreement with his master.

"Okay, pal," Brenden said, "let's take a walk and get some lunch. We've got to see the patients who pay our bills this afternoon. Maybe we can have some positive results back in our own stomping grounds."

The big dog stood and shook himself, and Brenden had the feeling that he was saying, *Don't worry about it, Master. It'll all work out. It always does.*

chapter seven

Brenden always tried to take the five o'clock ferry home so that he would be on time for an early dinner with his family, but today two patients kept him in the office until six thirty. He decided to place a call to "Bad News" Barnes before he headed home. He sensed that the distance between himself and Antwone Carver not only was based on the trauma the Marine had experienced, but also carried an overtone of racial mistrust that would make it difficult to develop a relationship.

He wondered how his friend Barnes had overcome this in his own life, both personally and professionally. Had Barnes's white patients questioned his capacity to treat them? Did he sometimes feel threatened or angry when he felt that whites were patronizing him, both because he was blind and because he was black? He was surprised to realize that he and Barnes had never really talked about any of these issues, and he found himself curious to discover what his friend would say.

The sonorous voice answered on the third ring.

"Hello," he said, "this is Dr. Barnes. May I help you?"

"I don't know," Brenden said. "It's after seven thirty back there. You may already be on your third drink and be no use to me at all."

"My second, young man," the voice said, "but at my size, I have an astounding capacity."

His tone then changed to a step-and-fetch-it kind of attitude, parodying the 1930s musicals. No one could ever be more self-deprecating. "Oh, golly gee, Dr. McCarthy," he said. "You mean, you really want the advice of a poor little ol' psychologist like me about your patient? Mm, mm, mm. Land sakes, I can't believe it."

Brenden laughed and parodied a British accent of his own. "I know it's quite remarkable," he said, "but sometimes we in the medical profession find it necessary to reach down to those of you who are less fortunate in order to help us solve a problem with which you, of the lower class, are more familiar."

Now Barnes laughed loudly, vibrating the crystal on Brenden's desk.

"Listen, Marvin," Brenden went on, "this is really serious. I'm calling about my pro bono case with Seattle Veterans Hospital. This guy, a Marine on his second tour in Iraq, was injured when an IED exploded on his Humvee. Now he's a paraplegic, including the possible loss of sexual function, suffering from post-traumatic stress disorder, and he seems completely closed off, either to a drug protocol or to any form of interactive therapy."

"That's interesting," the big man said. "It sounds like a couple of guys at this table, doesn't it? When we went blind, neither of us was reachable. I don't find this Marine's feelings to be unusual, do you?"

"It's not just that, Marvin," Brenden said. "I've only seen him once, but there seems to be a cultural divide, and even more, I have the feeling that it's going to be difficult for me to establish the kind of trust necessary to make the therapy useful. Do you get where I'm coming from?"

The big man took a long pull on his drink and sighed.

"The racial divide," he said. "A chasm wider than the Grand Canyon and getting wider. You know, Brenden," he went on reflectively, "I really think it was a lot easier in this country when the polarization of the races was more clear-cut. Now, with the success of affirmative action and the Civil Rights Amendment, prejudice has gone underground, and it's rooted deeply on both sides. I worry very much that we're void of effective leadership to continue to bring the issues forward in the minds of the American people. Look, I'm not trying to get on a soapbox or anything, but I can tell you that when I grew up during the sixties, the African-American community had real leadership. Now we have rap and bling and attitude, and that garbage can't do any of us any good. But I must say I'm encouraged by the election of Obama as president. There seems to be a change of attitude going on that's affecting not only this country but countries around the world. It makes you believe that something profound and grand just might be happening. To tell you the truth, Brenden, I'm praying about it, and I haven't done that for a long, long time. But back to your patient. Tell me about his family background."

"From what I've learned so far," Brenden said, "he never knew his father, so it's a matriarchal family. Eight kids, abject poverty, drugs, and gang violence. His life could have gone either way, but the Marine Corps became his family, and then he fell in love with his wife. I haven't met her, but I get the impression that she is a remarkable woman. He clearly has her on a pedestal."

The big man sounded thoughtful. "Here he is, flat on his back, having lost the Corps and believing that he's not a whole man anymore. Therapy won't be easy, Brenden, because somehow you're going to have to help him rebuild his sense of worth—and at the same time not minimize the problem. Remember when you came to see me for the first time? By sharing my story, I was able to create the kind of empathy that let us work together. This guy needs to understand that you've lived through the devastation of accidental disability and that your blindness, frankly, makes you color-blind."

Brenden drummed his fingers on the desk. "But will he buy into that idea, Marvin? I mean, does that sound too corny?"

"Do you believe it's true?" the big man asked. "Are you color-blind?"

"Sure," Brenden said. "You know I am."

"Well then, orient your therapy around your sincere beliefs, and then make sure that you gradually expose him to the successes that guys in wheelchairs all over the country are having. You also know there's been some promising research regarding in vitro fertilization that's allowing some spinal cord victims to still have families."

"I know that's true," Brenden said.

"We've come a long way," the big man said. "So make sure you gather all that data and have it ready to share with your patient."

"Any other thoughts?" Brenden asked, encouraged.

"I think you'll probably want to get him involved in some group sessions. They have them at the hospital, right?"

"Yes, they do," Brenden told the big man. "Apparently, with federal cutbacks, there is very little one-on-one time being offered."

Marvin snorted. "That drives me crazy, man. This stuff is so personal. I mean, when you're talking about something like sexual function, to share that with a group, at least in the beginning, makes real communication almost impossible. No one wants to be that open and intimate. There has to be one-on-one involvement with your therapist in order to set the foundations necessary for group participation. Boy oh boy, we've got to do better."

The two men were quiet for a minute. Eventually Barnes said, "Okay, well, try to get him involved. He very much believes in the Corps, so peer group engagement might be very useful. I also think that it's going to be important for you to spend some time treating the couple. His wife is still in Seattle, isn't she?"

"She's back and forth," Brenden said. "I found out from the

attending nurse that she's a teacher in San Diego, so while Carver is completing his physical therapy with us, his wife comes to visit as often as she can."

"Why didn't they put him in a hospital closer to home?" Barnes asked.

"I don't know," Brenden said. "Some kind of bureaucratic snafu based on how he was transported back to America."

"Well," Barnes said, "maybe it's just as well."

"What do you mean?" Brenden asked.

"He's in the hands of the psychiatrist best equipped to face his particular problem, isn't he?"

Brenden sighed. "I don't know, Marvin. I just don't know."

Brenden heard his friend's voice take on a tone of urgency.

"Listen, Brenden, one of the most important requirements in dealing with these guys is that you completely believe in what you're saying. It's not enough to just offer therapy, whether that's directive or analytical. You have to be in the business of offering hope, because that's the commodity these men are lacking. They've given up hope, quit on themselves, and quit believing that the system cares about them. You've got to be more proactive. It comes down to this: you have to be a missionary of hope, get involved, cross the line."

Again Brenden was quiet, and then he said, "I guess that's the way you treated me, right, Marvin?"

The big man chuckled. "You've got it, boy. You've figured out my trade secret. To be honest, I wasn't sure when I first met you that I could reach you, and based on the fact that later on you considered"—he paused—"you considered suicide, I had good reason to doubt the potential results; but I took a chance and launched into a proactive approach."

Brenden could hear the big man's voice take on a satisfied smile.

"And it worked. You're about the best-adjusted blind guy I know . . . outside of me, of course."

"Marvin," Brenden said, "in my professional opinion, you have an ego big enough for the whole state of Colorado."

"Let's not stop there, son," the big man said. "If you're going to believe in yourself, make it an ego the size of the whole country. You'll need that kind of confidence, especially if you're going to lift someone out of the depths of despair."

"Okay, Coach," Brenden said. "That was just what I needed, and now I'd better get on the ferry and head home to the family."

At the sound of the word *home*, Nelson stood, yawned, and stretched.

"Okay, my boy," Barnes said. "Give everyone a hug for me. Call me if you need me."

"Thanks, Marvin," Brenden said. "Thanks a lot."

chaptereight

Darla Carver was beginning to feel desperate. Her instinct as a woman and a wife was telling her that Antwone was pulling deeper and deeper inside himself, building a shell around his emotions that she feared was becoming impenetrable.

Over the last few days, he had been unwilling to speak of rehabilitation or coming home or, when she pressed him, to talk to her about his injuries, the war, or the loss of his fellow Marines. He just said, "Ain't nothin' to say, baby. Ain't nothin' to say."

She knew that she had to get back to San Diego and her teaching position—not just because she had a responsibility to her class and the school district, but because, frankly, they needed the money. She understood that Antwone would be on permanent disability, but she also knew that following rehab they would need to consider an alternative career for her young husband.

Though the doctor's grim diagnosis was certainly on her mind, she was more concerned with getting her husband out of his state of depression. She loved Antwone—that was something she was very sure of—and she was committed to him for life. She didn't deny the potential pain of a marriage without the love, comfort, and joy of sex, but she knew she needed to find a way to make Antwone understand that he would always be her husband and that she relied on him for love, strength, and support.

She decided to try to lift his spirits by bringing him the kind of dinner she knew he relished. There weren't many soul food stores in Seattle, but she did find one. She bought fried chicken, collard greens, candied yams, and biscuits and gravy, along with a cherry pie—his favorite—hoping the familiar food would draw him out and allow them to share a conversation she knew they needed to have.

There they were, in a stark conference room at the end of a hospital corridor. The nurses had tried to make it lovely, allowing her to put flowers on the table, even permitting them to share a bottle of wine. But right from the beginning Darla knew something was very wrong. Her husband may have been small in stature, but he always had a large appetite, especially when the food was so appetizing; but tonight he just picked at his food, and she had to struggle to make even simple conversation.

In their relationship, she was the person who had removed his reticence and shyness, making him a communicator on every important level. She knew that it was because he loved her, yet what she was feeling now frightened her to her very core.

The shell Antwone was building around himself included his heart, and as she sat across from him, studying his face, she couldn't figure out how to break through. Over the last couple of days, she had tried touch, smiles, a loving kiss, tender words, but nothing was working. Now tonight was turning out to be a disaster. She wanted to cry; she wanted him to put his arms around her and tell her everything would be all right. She wanted to wake up from this nightmare and get her husband back. She remembered as she studied his face how she had anticipated his homecoming every time he was overseas or in a training cycle. They enjoyed being physically active together, often dancing at clubs late into the night, and in the endlessly perfect San Diego weather, they went jogging, swimming, rollerblading. Shamelessly, she also thought about how they had spent whole days in bed—their lovemaking fueled by being so much in love. But now . . . What now?

She was surprised as Antwone pushed his food away and, for the first time that night, looked straight at her. Then she shivered, realizing the eyes across the table weren't expressing love. They were vacant and distant, as if a decision had been made that was going to shatter her life.

She heard her husband take a deep breath and waited, suspended, for the ax to fall—the verdict, the sentencing by her husband, the sole judge and jury. There was no life in his voice.

"Go home, Darla. Just go home and forget about me."

"No," she protested, rising and reaching across the table,

trying to hug him. "No. I love you, Antwone. I need you. What are you talking about?"

He disconnected her arms and gently pushed her away.

"I'm talking about a man who can't love you, Darla. I'm talking about a man who has nothing. No Marine Corps. No future. No love to give. Nothing."

"You're just being crazy, Antwone," she said. "You're just out of your head. You don't mean any of this. You don't know what you're saying. I love you, Antwone. I love you."

She saw the tears start to come to his eyes, and . . . And then she saw him angrily wipe them away.

"Listen, girl," he said, his voice taking on the resolve of a trained Marine on a mission, "I was never good enough for you anyway. Not smart enough. Not funny enough. Not handsome enough. Not anything enough. With the Corps and how much I loved you, we could have made it. We could have had a good life, but now there's nothing. I'm nothing, and you can't change that, no matter how much you love me."

She tried to hug him again, but this time he pushed her away hard enough to knock her off balance.

Involuntarily she cried out, not in pain but in shock and hurt. "What are you doing, Antwone?" she said. "I won't accept this. You don't believe what you're saying."

For a brief moment she saw his face soften and his expression change. Once again there was love in his eyes, a love so deep that it had to be forever, and all of this—all of this—had to be a bad dream. Nothing more than a bad dream.

"Go home, Darla," he said again. "Go home and start a new

life without me. With someone else—a whole person who can love you the way you deserve."

Before she had a chance to speak, he turned his wheelchair and his back on her and wheeled his way out of the room. She rose and followed him, not even feeling her feet touching the ground. Her eyes were on his back as she followed him to his room. Without turning to look at her, he wheeled his way through the door and closed it. She froze with her hand just above the knob.

Should she open the door and force her way into his room, his life, and his heart? *No,* She thought. *I can't do that. Antwone has to find his way back to me if we're ever going to have a chance to be happy. He has to decide he needs me. More importantly, he has to realize that I need him. I'll do what he says. I'll go home. I'll start to teach, but there is no one else for me but Antwone. I'll try again. I'll keep on trying. I'll never stop. I love him.*

ANTWONE SAT IN THE chair, his head in his hands, his back against the door. His body convulsed as the tears poured down his face. He was alone. He had lost—no, he had given away—the person who was his treasure, his whole life, and now he was empty of any human connection. Family didn't matter, the Corps was gone, and his heart had left the building as he heard Darla's shoes tapping their way down the hall, walking out of the hospital, walking out of his life.

chapter**nine**

Wow, what a rare morning, Brenden thought as the ferry chugged its way toward Seattle.

He and Nelson were out on the open deck to appreciate one of the rare pristine days the Northwest offers.

Appreciate the good stuff, Brenden reminded himself. *Don't ever take anything for granted.*

As the sun glistened off the water, he ruminated over the profile that his friend Barnes had suggested might fit his new patient, Antwone Carver.

The issue that worried him most—even beyond the patient's potential for PTSD—was his own ability to establish trust and cross the void Barnes had described as the racial divide. He had treated ethnically diverse patients in the past, but never someone coming from the kind of inner-city background and family dysfunction indicated in Antwone's profile.

So how to begin? Barnes had suggested that sharing his own story might be helpful, and Brenden agreed, but since Carver had not even shown a willingness to begin therapy, Brenden believed that he had to approach the young Marine in a sort of obtuse manner.

WHEN HE AND NELSON got settled in his office in Madison Tower later that morning, he called Kat.

"Hi, beautiful," he said when she came on the line. "How busy are you this morning?"

"I'm okay," she said. "Are you trying to set up a romantic lunch?"

Brenden laughed. "I haven't got time for that today, dear, but I do need your help. Can you meet me at the hospital and bring along my basketball DVD?"

"Oh, you mean Showtime and the Lakers?"

"That's the one, babe. I think it might be helpful for me to share with my new patient. Oh, and about that romantic lunch, if you get here by noon, I think I might actually have time to have lunch with you."

"Okay, big fella," she said, laughing. "See you in two hours."

They ate at a small French restaurant down by the wharf called Andre's, which featured a delicious Provence-style preparation of sand dabs with delicate green beans and red skin potatoes. Over the meal, Brenden explained his problem in trying to establish communication with Antwone Carver. Kat was extremely supportive.

"Listen," she said, "you have a distinct advantage. Because you're blind, it won't take long for this guy to figure out that you are probably the single most unprejudiced person in the world. And I'm sure that every hurt person wants to find someone to communicate with, especially if they are feeling desperate."

When lunch was over, they shared a cab and a kiss before Brenden and Nelson went back to work.

"See you at home," she said as the man and the dog climbed out of the cab.

Brenden's smile said it all.

WHEN HE ARRIVED AT Seattle Veterans Hospital that afternoon, Brenden was surprised to learn from the nurse on duty that Corporal Carver's wife had left town. One of the nurses had left him a note at the station mentioning that Mrs. Carver was terribly upset but wouldn't talk about what had happened.

"Uh-oh," Brenden said to Nelson, "either this guy will be even more closed off, or he'll be open to talk to me. Let's go find out."

He found Antwone in the recreation room, sitting in his wheelchair in front of a window and listening to music through earphones. The nurse had to tap the man on the shoulder to get his attention.

"Corporal Carver," she said, "Dr. McCarthy is here to see you."

No response came from the guy in the chair, so Brenden plowed ahead.

"I brought you something," he said.

The man still didn't look at him.

"A real treasure," Brenden went on. "The Showtime Lakers."

He produced the DVD and held it out to Carver, who couldn't help but take it.

"Yes, sir," Brenden said. "Showtime—when B-ball was at its best—eighty-six. Worthy and Rambis up front; the captain, Kareem Abdul-Jabbar, in the middle with Byron Scott; and the Magic Man, Earvin 'Magic' Johnson, at his best, running the show. Then they came off the bench with people like lock-down defender Michael Cooper and Mr. Enthusiasm, Mychal Thompson. They were something, weren't they? You never really got to see them play, did you, Antwone? I mean, you were too young."

"Just seen highlights," the man said.

"Well, you'll love this video because it's narrated by Chick Hearn, the great Lakers announcer, and I think it really captures the team concept. The interviews on the video are really awesome. For those guys, team was everything—I bet a lot like the Marines. Hey, do you mind if I sit down?" he asked, as if he hadn't come there with that intention.

Carver nodded and Brenden pushed right through.

"Find the chair, Nelson," Brenden said. "Find the chair, boy."

The dog put his nose right on the seat of the chair Brenden wanted, and Carver couldn't help but acknowledge it.

"That's cool, man. I mean, the dog finding a chair like that. That is really cool."

"I told you," Brenden said. "He's special. Say hello to Antwone, Nelson," Brenden told the big dog.

Nelson wagged his tail and gave the man in the wheelchair a sniff.

"Pat him," Brenden encouraged Antwone. "That's what he wants, just some affection."

The Marine reached out tentatively and touched the dog on the head.

"No, I mean really give him a good pat," Brenden pressed. "You know, rub his ears or something. He wants to be your friend."

The blind man heard Carver ruffle the black Lab's ears and then heard the dog put his paw up on the man's leg.

"He wants you to shake hands with him," Brenden said, realizing that Antwone couldn't feel Nelson's paw on his knee. The doctor sensed that the man was smiling despite himself. He heard him pick up Nelson's paw.

"You're a real cool dog," he said to Nelson.

"He knows that," Brenden told the Marine. "He knows he's special. It's because he has a purpose."

The master snapped his fingers and called Nelson to lie down next to his chair.

"I suppose that's what we're all looking for, don't you think—a sense of purpose?"

"It don't matter when you're not good for anything," Carver said, "when you're half a Marine and half a man."

"Sometimes half is good enough," Brenden said. "I felt like you do when I went blind, you know. I was climbing a mountain in Colorado and felt like I was at the top of the world. The last thing I saw was a beautiful bald eagle flying free, and then my feet slipped on some loose stuff they call scree. It's really just rock. I fell, hit my head, destroyed the optic nerve, and, well, here I am, Blinky McCarthy."

"There wasn't anything the doctors could do?" Carver asked. "To fix your eyes, I mean?"

"Nope," Brenden said. "I'm as blind as a bat, and it's gonna stay that way."

"How did you handle it?" Carver asked.

"Not very well," Brenden told him. "Everything went dark in my life. The girl I thought loved me dumped me. I hated being around blind people in the rehab center, and I had no idea what I was going to do with my life. I was studying to be an orthopedic surgeon, but now . . ."

"But you're a psychiatrist," Carver said. "That's still a doctor, right?"

"Yes, it is, Antwone. There've only been a couple of us blind guys who have become psychiatrists. It's not easy, but you can do it. I've figured out over the last few years that you can do almost anything if you want it enough. The thing is, you have to make a decision to want it. Take a look back at your own life. Haven't there been things you wanted and couldn't get, and then been surprised because you did?"

Brenden sensed the man look down at the floor in concentration and then raise his eyes back to the doctor's face.

"I used to believe that," he said, "but all the things I wanted I didn't get, or I lost."

"What do you mean?" Brenden asked.

"Listen, man, I was everything in basketball," Carver said. "During high school, all-city, I averaged twenty and ten, you know? Twenty points and ten assists a game. Probably was the best point guard, at least in California. Would have had college offers if I hadn't gotten in trouble. Stupidest thing I ever did—stealing a car. So I spent time in juvie, and then, well, the Corps came along, and I figured *that* was a better team to belong to."

"Antwone, I sense that you think the Marines have abandoned you. Is that what you believe?"

"No, man," Carver said, agitated. "The Corps didn't abandon me. They just don't need me anymore. Not like this."

"But you're one of them," Brenden pointed out. "They admire you. I know that a bunch of the guys have visited while you've been here. They even brought a cake, I heard."

"Yeah," Carver said. "It's called an Alive Day cake. You get one to honor the fact that you're alive. I mean, when everybody's sure you're gonna stay that way."

"Well," Brenden said carefully, "that means they care about you, doesn't it?"

"But I'm no use to anybody," Carver said, returning to his original theme. "Not like this."

"Wait a minute," Brenden said, "these guys are your pals. They came all the way from San Diego to see you."

"That's nothing but sympathy, man," Carver went on bitterly. "They're just visiting a brother because they feel sorry for him."

Brenden continued to argue gently. "I don't think that's true, Antwone. I think it's because they admire your sacrifice and believe that once a Marine, always a Marine. I suppose that's what the cake is all about—being alive and being a Marine.

"Listen," Brenden went on earnestly, "I've had the chance to talk to World War II vets who have gone on to have great lives, and they still believe that first, foremost, and always they're Marines. I think Marines are maybe the most special brotherhood in the world—at least to a civilian—and I think you're lucky to be one of them."

Carver was quiet, so Brenden tried to lead him a little more.

"You know, Antwone, everybody wants to belong. All of us have a basic need to be part of something outside ourselves. Nobody can make it living in isolation. We need to know that people love us and care about us and that we're part of the human community."

"It's a tough world out there," Carver said finally, "and if you're half a man, you don't have a place in it. Back in my neighborhood, if people knew you were in a chair, it'd just make it easier for them to rip you off."

"You really think so?" Brenden asked.

"Mm-hm," Carver said. "That's the way it works, man. That's the way it always has."

Brenden paused a moment, reflecting. "So tell me a bit about your childhood."

"Childhood?" Carver said. "I didn't have a childhood, man. I had a survival-hood. Christmas didn't mean nothing. Birthdays, nothing. We didn't have anything. Eight kids. I don't know how many daddies. Project housing. Rats and gangs. Drugs and pimps. You survive by staying out of the way when you can and fighting when you have to."

"So do you still keep in touch with your family?" Brenden asked.

"I was fourth in age," Carver said, "right in the middle. I've got a couple of brothers doin' time; one dead in a gangland drive-by; two sisters with two kids each, no daddies; and two that are doing okay. Not very good odds, but that's the way it is in the hood."

Brenden observed that most of the physical signs he had noted earlier relating to PTSD were evident in the man's behavior—the agitation, the nervousness, the jumpy expression, the fast speech, the out-of-control finger tapping. And most of the emotional signs were there, too, including depression and anxiety. Brenden decided this was not the time to bring up the sudden departure of Corporal Carver's wife. Better to leave that for another session. He hoped the Marine wasn't even thinking of their time together as therapy, but maybe just two guys having a conversation. *Sometimes that's the best way,* he thought, *when you don't make it technically a session. Sometimes you get far better results.*

"Listen," he said. "Check out the video. There are DVD players in the TV room. I'll come back tomorrow afternoon, and we'll talk about it. Maybe we can watch it together. As an old point guard, I'm sure you can tell me some of the inside ways Magic plays the game that other people miss."

"I'll watch it," Carver said.

"Wonderful," Brenden said. "By the way," he went on casually, "now that you're a patient of mine, I'd like to recommend a course of medication that might be help—"

Carver interrupted him and snapped, "I'm not taking any of that garbage. No drugs for me."

"Antwone," Brenden said easily, "like a lot of guys who come home from the war, I think you're struggling with a condition called post-traumatic stress disorder. Have you ever heard of it?"

"Yeah, I've heard of it," Carver said. "They talked about it a lot during training and when we were in country."

"Do you know anyone who suffers with it?" Brenden asked.

"A few," Carver said. "We had a few guys in my unit, but that ain't me, man. That ain't me."

"I think you *are* one of those guys," Brenden told him gently, "and I really believe the medication can be very helpful. Look, Antwone, it's totally up to you, but I think you'll find that it really makes a big difference to your overall sense of well-being. I hope you'll consider going on the medicine, let's say for a month. By that time you'll be out of here and under someone else's care, and you can discuss it with your new doctor. But I want you to know we've had tremendous success getting men back on track, and I think you could definitely be one of them."

Now Carver's eyes were directly on the blind man's face. Brenden could sense that the look was challenging.

"Will I start to sleep better, Doc? Will it take away the nightmares? Will I be able to play hoops, dance with my wife, have sex, and feel like a man again? Will your drugs do all that, Doc?" Antwone's voice seethed with pain and loathing.

Brenden waited a few seconds before responding. "There's no guarantee, Antwone," he said. "I can only tell you that, professionally, I've seen some wonderful results."

"How many pills a day will I have to take?" Antwone asked. "I hate taking pills."

"Well, let's see," Brenden said, "I'd like to start you off with two medicines. One of them is a mood stabilizer."

The man laughed. "There's nothing you can do about my moods, Doc. No drug is going to make a difference in the way I feel."

"We'll see," Brenden said, going on. "And the second drug is for the anxiety I believe you're feeling."

Again the man in the wheelchair laughed. "No anxiety here, man. Nothing to be anxious about. When you don't have a reason to live anymore, there's no reason to be anxious. Nobody's shooting at me, and nobody's loving me."

Right on cue, Nelson's tail thumped the floor, as if he had been listening to the whole conversation.

Brenden smiled. "Well, Antwone, I think you're wrong. Nelson doesn't agree with you. I'll bet he can love you. He taught me about love after the accident that left me blind."

Brenden sensed the man's acknowledgment, even if it was grudging, so he moved on to describe the drug protocol.

"So for anxiety, I think we'll begin with Ativan. It's a proven medicine, and people have had astounding success with it. For the depression you're probably feeling, I've seen great results with Zoloft. Now, with the Zoloft we'll begin with a low dosage for a week, and then if you're not having any reaction—and I don't expect you will—we'll increase it. Okay?"

"Okay, Doc," the man relented, surprising Brenden. "That'll be fine. Let's try the drugs."

"Fine," Brenden said. "I'll check in with you in the next couple of days. Hope you enjoy the video."

"The Magic Man," Carver said.

"Earvin 'Magic' Johnson."

"Yeah, Doc, he was the man. Thanks."

"Say good-bye to Antwone, Nelson," Brenden said. This time when the dog came forward, Brenden heard the Marine rubbing the dog's ears without any prompting.

When Brenden returned to his office, he sat at the old desk, pondering his feelings on the session. Because their first visit had been a confrontation, Brenden had not taken a full history or mental status exam, but he felt that this second exchange had given him what he needed to reflect on the patient's chart. Antwone Carver was clearly mentally stable under the mental status criteria. His memory was excellent, and Brenden did not feel that the man would have any trouble dealing with abstract concepts. His concentration was excellent, and his focus, though affected by PTSD, was reasonably consistent as they moved from subject to subject. The question was whether Brenden would be able to create a therapeutic connection with Antwone Carver. The jury was still out on that, he decided.

He spoke into his cassette machine: "I believe it is possible for me to forge an appropriate therapeutic alliance with the patient, Antwone Carver. Trust will be the important question, but I believe it is possible because the patient is so vulnerable at this time in his history. I may be able to become a surrogate support system for him, and I intend to try to use a number of concepts to obtain his trust."

Turning off the machine, McCarthy reached down and patted the big dog. "I could use a little therapy myself, Nelson," he said. "Let's surprise the family and call it a day early. What do you think?"

The dog stood, stretched, and shook, as if he completely understood what his master was saying, and Brenden mused that he probably did.

chapterten

The heavy morning fog was back, compressing the sound of their breathing, making the exertion take on a surreal effect. Brenden and Kat rode the tandem bike up the long hill at the east end of the island, working together to engage every erg of energy, propelling the machine over the top of the hill and then, like a runaway train, picking up speed as the bike rolled down the other side. The wind roared through the ear holes of their helmets as they hunkered down over the handlebars, getting the most from the descent.

Kat was a superb captain on the front of the tandem, controlling their speed with the delicacy of a surgeon as she used her hand brakes and drum brake just enough to maintain the line between control and reckless abandon.

Brenden also understood his job, keeping his body centered and always being alert to any signal Kat might give him through their pedaling. It was important for the biker at the rear of the tandem to be aggressive in his effort, but also to make sure that in working for the best performance he did not move the bike offline by trying to pull too hard with his upper body. Because Brenden was probably eighty pounds heavier than Kat, this issue was even more important. But as in everything else they did together, the couple loved their particular sense of team and common goal.

They were training for the Chilly Hilly bike race that would be held on the island next winter. They had won the tandem couples division three times, and they had no intention of giving up their crown. Along with their daily individual exercise, they tried to share their bike riding twice a week—once when Brenden took a short day at the office, and always on Saturday mornings.

They were able to find a responsible teenage girl to babysit the children, which allowed them to go out after their ride for a long, lingering breakfast. More than any other time during the week, this Saturday morning biking and breakfast was the real nurturing of their relationship. No kids, just time to remember why they were in love.

Brenden understood why he loved Kat, but he figured he was the luckiest man in the world that, for reasons he could not understand, she felt the same way. He was thinking of that at the end of their ride as they sat at a table in Jack's, a restaurant with the best omelets on the island, fresh, buttery croissants that melted in your mouth, and some of Seattle's best coffee.

Life on a Saturday morning just couldn't get any better. As Kat poured Brenden his second cup of coffee from a pot the waiter had left on the table, the grateful husband found himself thinking about Antwone Carver and his wife. Could they find the same kind of lasting happiness that he shared with Kat, or would the emotional challenges and physical limitations, including the added complication of sexual dysfunction, destroy the critical balance of love and passion necessary for a marriage to be sustained and grow? He decided to broach the subject with Kat, but first he needed to make her understand the ethical implications of their conversations about Antwone.

"Do you remember the Marine I told you about whose spine was shattered by an IED?"

"Sure," Kat said. "I've thought about it a lot since you brought it up—the devastation, I mean, for him personally and for them as a couple."

"I need your advice," Brenden went on, "but this conversation has to remain completely confidential. You understand, right? Because of the client-patient relationship. Technically, I'm not supposed to talk to anyone—even my spouse—about my clients, but I trust you to keep this information just between us."

"Yes," she said. "Certainly I understand."

"Okay," Brenden said. "Well, his wife went back to San Diego. She was very upset when she left, or at least that's what the nurses who were on duty have told me. I haven't brought it up yet with Carver, because I wanted to talk to you first."

"Me?" Kat queried. "How come? Why me?"

"Because you married me." Brenden smiled. "Because you had the courage to marry a guy who felt that there wasn't much to live for, who felt that his disability had made him worthless to anybody, most importantly himself."

"Listen, baby," Kat said, taking on a tone more serious than Brenden expected, "I waited all my life for you, and I knew the first day I met you, when you came skiing and I saw you in Hal O'Leary's office, that you were the person I wanted to grow old with, sleep with, have children with, and share mornings like this with. I love you. Now, do you need any more strokes for a Saturday morning, or is that quite enough?"

"Okay, Kat," Brenden said, laughing. "You know how much I love you, but what I want you to talk to me about are the adjustments you had to make around my disability. I mean, are there times when my blindness is a burden for you?"

Kat considered. "Well," she said, "there are times when I have to take it into consideration—like when we're out in public, and I have to remember to guide you when Nelson's not around, or when I need to set your closet up just right so you can find what you need, or make sure that you know where everything is in a strange place. But that's just learning how to make a system work, and none of that has anything to do with who you are as a person or how I feel about you. Our relationship doesn't have anything to do with your disability. It just has to do with our uniqueness, our chemistry, our love."

"Sure, Kat, but there have to be things that bother you,"

Brenden pressed. "Things that create—how should I put this?—things that cause a difference in the way we love and the way other couples share."

"That's exactly right," Kat said. "To put it in a simple way you could share with your client, I'd say that our specialness is made up of the elements that make us different from anyone else. We talk more than other couples do. I mean, we have to. I can't give you one of those looks that kill because you'll miss it, so I have to be more open about telling you exactly how I feel. The way we ride our bike so intimately together, you know how special that is. And your faith in God and his purpose for your life shows in everything you do. I love the way you teach our children about the senses and the way you've come to appreciate the world—like the other day, taking Nelson to Brian's school. How many dads get to do that?"

Kat moved her fork around on her plate. "Look, let me add this. Okay, sure, there are times when we're going somewhere, and I dress just so. Certainly I'd like it—no, I'd love it—if you could see me and understand that I've dressed just for you. But it's okay."

"I know, Kat. I think about that sometimes—"

She interrupted. "But I always know you appreciate me, and I know that you see me as beautiful inside out, rather than outside in."

"The outside's not bad," Brenden said, meaning it. "Not bad at all."

"You bet, buster," Kat said. "I am one great package."

She took his hand in hers across the table. "Brenden, I believe God sent you to me, that you were picked especially for me, and I'd like to think that you feel the same way."

"Of course I do, Kat," Brenden said earnestly. "You know that's how I feel."

"My point is, Brenden," she went on, "the old adage is really true. Love does conquer all, and when we love, we accept the idea that part of what we care about is each other's imperfection. Now, if you want to think of disability as imperfection, at least for this conversation, you can understand what I'm trying to say."

"But when a disability is imposed on you by accident," Brenden asked, "or in this case, by war, relationship can be lost in the starkness of adjustment, can't it?"

"Absolutely," Kat said, "and that probably means you're going to have to talk to Mrs. Carver to understand where she's coming from."

"That's what I thought," Brenden agreed. "But not yet. I have to find a way to establish trust with Antwone and rebuild some of his psychological foundation before I begin working with him on reestablishing his relationship with his wife. You see, Kat, I had to begin to love myself before you could love me."

"I suppose that's true," Kat acknowledged. "But Mrs. Carver loved Antwone before his injury, and I don't think a woman who commits her heart gives up on a guy just because he's hurt. We're a unique species, Brenden, we women. When a woman loves a man—I mean, really loves him—she adapts, no matter what."

Brenden leaned across the table and kissed his wife lightly

on the cheek. "You certainly do," he said. "You've been adapting to me for years."

"And it's not easy, boy," she said, giving him that Kat smile that even a blind man could see. "What's the Billy Joel song? 'Just the Way You Are'? Well, that's how I feel." And she confirmed it, singing quietly, "I love you just the way you are." Brenden joined in for a few lines, savoring their time together.

Then he reached down and touched his stomach. "Boy, am I full—and now we have to bike home."

"Slowly," Kat said. "Very slowly."

DARLA CARVER HADN'T SLEPT. As far as she could tell, she hadn't slept for days, and when she looked in the mirror that morning, in the bathroom of her apartment in San Diego, the face that looked back at her was tired, worn, and sad. *My broken heart is all over my face,* she thought as she studied her reflection. *But I can't give up on Antwone. I just can't give up.*

For the thousandth time she tried to decide whether she should go back to Seattle and pound on his door and his heart, or give him the space to miss her and work out this nightmare for himself. She couldn't decide. Her husband had pushed her away. She understood that, but she also knew that in some way he was trying to save her from his perception of what her life would be like with him.

Antwone had always been a fighter, and in one way or another he had always reached for the higher ground of life, whether it was on the basketball court or in the Marine Corps.

His mother's persistent faith in the unwavering love of Jesus had made an impact on Antwone, perhaps more than he knew. She believed his character had been shaped by that faith, and as a result, he would overcome his disability. She could only hope that in time he would realize he needed that love—from Jesus and from her. The tough part was, would he ever believe that she needed him?

Staring at the exhausted face in her mirror, she had no answer when it came to convincing him. *I'll just have to be patient,* she thought. *I just have to believe in love.*

"I hope so," she said out loud and then turned it into a prayer. "God, please grant me the strength to get through this, and please bring Antwone back to me. Amen."

ANTWONE CARVER WASN'T PRAYING at all. He was consumed by self-pity, loathing, and rage. All he could think about was that life had once again dealt him a terrible blow. The explosion was just another in a chain of events that designated him as a loser. Black, poor, short, and disabled—unable to fulfill even the basic role of a husband and, someday, a father. Antwone Jamal Carver was worthless to himself, the Corps, Darla, and anyone else.

So what to do about it? He sat in his wheelchair and pondered that problem. He didn't have a solution completely worked out yet, but at least he had something to think about, and he became consumed, thinking about nothing else.

chapter eleven

Something was nagging at the back of Brenden McCarthy's mind.

It was that little voice people are always talking about; the little voice that arose out of personal instinct and was cultivated through years of experience and an innate survival mechanism. A voice that told him God was trying to guide him.

That little voice had served him well throughout his life. It let Brenden know that Kat was the only woman for him, and it gave him a special insight into understanding people and developing the intimacy necessary to be a competent psychiatrist.

Now that little voice at the back of his head was telling him that something was not quite right about Antwone Carver. On the one hand, the Marine was unwilling to enter any form of therapy. The guy had made that crystal clear. Why then was he so willing to accept a drug protocol to treat PTSD? It didn't make sense. As Brenden and Nelson made the ferry crossing on the following Monday morning, the doctor listened to that little voice, knowing that he needed to figure out Carver's true motivation.

As he sipped his coffee with the big dog lying at his feet, listening to the comforting throb of the ferry's engine, Brenden speculated about how he would go about trying to break down the barriers in order to engage Carver in treatment intervention. He knew his time with the Marine would be limited. The VA system worked to get these guys back to their homes and families, and that was the way it should be. Brenden understood that it would be up to someone else to carry on the long-term, meaningful work that would hopefully bring Carver back as a healthy member of the civilian community. But he knew it was important for him to set the groundwork that would allow the injured man the chance to gain a foothold on his future. The first few weeks were critical. He decided that his best course was to talk to Antwone in practical terms.

The truth was, for Carver to get the maximum benefit available under his service disability, the psychiatrist's diagnosis would seal the deal. Brenden figured that he could make this point strongly to Carver, even if the man thought the time they would be spending together was basically worthless. That was often the case, Brenden mused, when people began therapy. No one wants to face the possibility that a psychiatrist could be helpful, because in agreeing to that concept you are accepting the idea that you need help, which is difficult in the case of military personnel.

Dr. Harrison had told him during their lunch that the macho soldiers' code of bravery—and their intense training in how to survive independently—made it much harder for professionals to convince them that any form of therapy was a good idea. Harrison had gone on to say that overcoming this barrier with Antwone Carver would probably be the most frustrating part of McCarthy's job.

Brenden also knew that the newness of tremendous dependence on other people—to accomplish even the most basic tasks—was a harsh lesson in humility. Fear and pride had to be pushed aside so that learning could commence. Antwone's military training taught him about independent survival, but his childhood faith in God's sacrificial love would show him how to start living again.

Brenden could only hope that Bad News Barnes was right, and that his own disability and the adjustments he had made could serve both as an inspiration and as a demonstration to Carver that he could continue to have a full and vital life.

Brenden and Nelson arrived at the hospital, and as always, the big black Lab had quickly acclimated to his new work surroundings. Brenden never even had to issue a command. Nelson simply entered the building, went straight to the elevators, put his nose on the Up button, and guided his master inside, where Brenden selected the fourth-floor button. When they got off the elevator, Nelson wound his way down the corridor, stopped at Brenden's office door, waited until the man put the key in the lock, and then guided his master to his chair and lay down with a contented sigh that said, *Now, wasn't that good, Master?*

Brenden asked the duty nurse to have Carver come to his office after he finished his course of physical therapy. Thank goodness the Marine was used to the regimen of taking orders, and he arrived promptly at eleven o'clock, though Brenden could tell right away Carver still had no interest in seeing him.

The doctor tried to break the ice, asking Carver if he'd had a chance to watch the DVD on Magic Johnson and the Lakers.

"Yeah," Carver said.

"So, Antwone," Brenden said casually, "what do you think it was that made Magic Johnson such a unique basketball player?"

Carver was on safe ground, so he chose to answer the question.

"First of all, man, he must have had eyes in the back of his head or had, like, Superman vision, you know? I mean, it was almost like he could look through walls or something. Some of the passes he made, man—I don't know how he could see someone open, but the ball would just be at the right place, and it would be a slam dunk for Worthy or a skyhook by Cap or that sweet Byron Scott jump shot—all set up by the Magic Man."

"Then you'd say that Magic made everybody better?"

"Oh, no question, man. When you played with Magic, some of it rubbed off." Carver paused and then cleared his throat. "So why'd you ask me to come here, Doc? I told you already, I'm not interested in any therapy mumbo jumbo, so unless we're going to talk hoop, I think it's about time for me to go back to my room."

"Look, here's the deal," Brenden said. "When you get out of here, you're going to want the most money you can get around your injuries, right?"

"Mm-hm," the man said. "One thing for sure," he went on, "I've earned the right to some of Uncle's dollars. He took the best I have. I deserve something back."

"That's right," Brenden agreed. "And I really want you to get it, but you're going to have to talk with me for a while so I can write up the report on PTSD, confirming the diagnosis. It won't be too painful, I promise you. You might even feel better."

"Humph," the man acknowledged. "Okay, Doc," he finally said, resigned, "what do you want to know?"

Brenden sat back in his chair and assumed the casual body position Kat had recommended. He also made sure that he was facing directly toward the sound of Antwone's voice, knowing that even if he couldn't see him, it was very important that Carver felt that Brenden was really interested in what he had to say.

It was good that Brenden remembered what it had been like to be a sighted person, and those memories helped him greatly in making the important visual connections his patients needed.

"Okay, here's the first question for us to talk about. Who is Antwone Carver?"

The response came quicker than Brenden expected.

"He's nothing," the man said. "He used to be something, but now he's nothing."

"Why do you feel that way?" Brenden asked.

"Man, isn't it obvious?" Carver said, the anger flaring. "You more than just blind, man? Are you stupid, too? I'm in this chair. I'm going to be in it for the rest of my life. What kind of a life am I gonna have now that I can't walk? I can't do nothing for myself now."

"Nothing at all, Antwone?"

"Here it is, man. I got my GED in the Corps, so I'm not qualified for anything. And there's not much else that really interests me. I'm never going to be an office type. I'm blue collar, man, all the way, and there just ain't many jobs, you know, for a blue-collar brother with no skills. You hear what I'm saying, jack? This rehabilitation don't mean nothing. Rehabilitate to do what, man? Pick up my checks the first of the month? That's as far as rehab's going to take me."

"Isn't it possible," Brenden suggested, "that you really don't have the whole picture? That you're underestimating yourself or maybe feeling just a little sorry for yourself?"

"What? You don't think I have a good reason?"

"Oh, you've got plenty of good reasons, Antwone, but what good does that do you? Remember, you can't change your yesterdays, but you can do something with your today and your tomorrows. I think that kind of decision is up to you. Look, you've already proved you've got what it takes to make it in the world. You told me about your family, how dysfunctional it was, and yet you made a decision to try for something better. You chose the Corps, and you married Darla. Why can't something like that happen again?"

"I told you," Carver said, raising his voice. "Because there's nothing left."

"You mean your legs," Brenden said. "Because you can't walk and because you believe you can't really love? Listen, Antwone, do you think love is sex? I mean, do you think they're the same thing?"

"What are you talking about, Doc? Between a man and a woman, there ain't no love without sex."

"I don't agree with you," Brenden responded. "There's a whole lot about love that doesn't happen in the bedroom. There's a lot more to being a human being than just sex. Remember the question I asked you? Let's stay on that point for a while. I asked you, who is Antwone Carver, deep down inside?"

Carver didn't answer, so Brenden prompted, "Is he a guy who loves his family? I know they have a lot of problems, but do they matter to you, Antwone?"

Brenden heard the motion as the man nodded.

"Do you think your mother's proud of you? I mean, because of the Corps and Darla and everything?"

"Yeah," the man said. "She's proud."

"Did you help her with some of her bills when you were getting combat pay?"

"I guess so. Sure," the man said. "I gave her some dough every once in a while."

"And I bet you've helped your brothers and sisters, too, right?"

"Sometimes. What else are you gonna do? People need help, you give it. What's that mean? It doesn't mean you're worth anything. Maybe it's just because you want them . . ." He stopped, so Brenden finished the sentence with a question.

"Do you mean you want them to love you? Is that what you mean?"

No response came from the Marine, so Brenden pushed on. "So what about the Corps? The guys in your unit. Do you help them out?"

"That's different," Carver said. "That's the Corps, man. You know. Of course you help a brother. It's the Marines. We're all brothers."

"So what do you think the Lakers felt when they played with Magic? What do you think that was all about?"

"It was team, you know?" Antwone said. "They were all part of a team."

"So is it reasonable to think that being a member of a team is part of who Antwone Carver is?"

"I don't know," Carver said.

"And your relationship with Darla—that's being part of something more than yourself, isn't it?"

"She's my heart," Carver said, dropping his eyes. "She's everything."

"And, Antwone," Brenden pressed, sensing an important opportunity, "does she feel the same way about you?"

"You mean, does she love me?" Carver said quietly. "Yeah, she loves me."

"Why? Why does she love you?"

Carver didn't answer, and Brenden let the silence hang between them.

Finally he said, "If your wife was here in this room with us, I have a feeling that she'd say she loves you because of who you are, because you have qualities that make you Antwone Carver—and that Antwone Carver is a valuable person with a lot to offer. Look," Brenden went on, "between now and when I see you in a couple of days, would you make a list of the reasons Darla loves you? Write them down, and then ask yourself the question: 'If Darla can feel this way about me, isn't it possible that I can feel good about myself?'"

Immediately Brenden felt the man pushing back. "There's no reason for Darla to love me anymore," he said, his head still down. "Because there's nothing left to love."

"I think you're wrong," Brenden told the young Marine. "I believe when you think about it, you'll figure out there's a lot about you that is pretty darn special."

Carver didn't acknowledge the last comment, but Brenden knew he heard it.

As he heard the man move his wheelchair toward the door, Brenden asked, "So, Antwone, how're you doing on the medication? Any problems? Any reaction?"

"With the drugs?" Antwone said. "No problem, Doc. No problem at all."

"It takes a few days for them to take effect," Brenden told him, "but I think you'll find that the results will be very helpful."

"I hope so," the man said as he wheeled through the door. "I'm counting on it."

chapter twelve

Brenden sat with earphones clamped on his head as his computer program read the text of a book called *The Devil's Sandbox*. He needed to try to develop at least a cursory knowledge of the Iraqi conflict and the circumstances under which the Marines were forced to operate. The age-old hatred between Shias, Sunnis, and Kurds; the tribal structure; the fledgling government—all of it placing America's finest, the Marines, in a role that seemed, at best, to be miscast.

As a civilian, Brenden believed the U.S. Marine Corps was the greatest fighting force in the history of the world, but it seemed to him that it functioned best when understanding its true enemy. He expected Antwone Carver to talk about a soldier's disillusionment with the role he was asked to fulfill, and

Brenden was preparing—as his therapist—to be able to empathize with the patient's frustrations.

Kat had seen her husband this way before as he struggled to get inside the mind-set of his patients, and she understood it would be a long night for her man. So with a gentle kiss on the cheek and a soft "good night," she went to bed, leaving Brenden to try to understand a complex problem that had clearly been exacerbated by the United States.

THE NURSE DELIVERED ANTWONE Carver's nightly pill, and the man's ritual was working well. Placing the pill in his mouth, he tucked it into the back of his cheek as he quickly drank a small cup of water. Then after a polite "good night" to the nurse as she walked out the door, he removed the soggy pill from his mouth and placed it—along with all the others he'd been saving—in his shaving kit.

My stash is getting bigger, he thought to himself. *Not long now. Not too long.*

THE NEXT MORNING WHEN Carver wheeled into McCarthy's office, Nelson didn't even have to be prompted to say hello. He did it naturally, and the response from the young Marine was becoming almost as natural. If you were watching, you would note that the young soldier actually seemed glad to see the big black dog.

A nice breakthrough, Brenden observed, calling Nelson back to the side of his chair. *Everyone wants to be loved. That's what I'm hoping for—that everyone wants to be loved.*

This morning Carver seemed more open, even somewhat enthused to begin their conversation.

"So what are we going to talk about today, Doc? What part of my mind are you going to try to blow?"

"I want to know more about the Corps," Brenden said. "About what it really means for you to be a Marine. Let's start with why you joined."

"Easy," Carver said. "It wasn't no choice."

"Oh, you mean because of the trouble you were in?" Brenden suggested. "But why the Corps instead of the Army or Navy or some other branch of the service?"

"I love the posters," Carver said. "You know: 'The Marines want you'; 'The few, the proud, the brave' . . . all that stuff. It seemed cool to be part of something that was special."

"Did you always want to be special?" Brenden asked.

"I don't know, man," Carver said. "I hadn't really thought about it."

"Well, you wanted to make it in the NBA. That's special. Since you've been in the Corps, you've had a spotless record. I think somewhere inside Antwone Carver, you want to be part of something that matters, something that counts. So is that what you got out of the Corps?"

Carver laughed. "It's funny. I liked it right from the beginning," he said. "Even the discipline. When a lot of guys hated the DIs—"

"You mean the drill instructors?" Brenden clarified.

"Tops," Carver said. "Sergeants. I loved them. You see, I figured they couldn't make it tough enough for me. Coming from the streets, where I come from, I could handle anything they threw at me. The hikes. The hill climbs. The live ammo tests. Even simple stuff like parade, ground, and inspection. Even the hand-to-hand combat, when the other guys figured I was too little and couldn't handle myself. When it came to basic training, man, it was cake. I loved it. And when I got out of Parris Island and the sergeant congratulated me, I put on the dress uniform, and I felt awesome, really awesome. And then they sent us over to that pit."

"Iraq?" Brenden asked.

"Yeah," Carver said, the derision clear in his tone. "It isn't a fair fight, you know."

"Tell me how it's not fair."

"When you're in country," Carver said, "you just don't know who to trust. It's a lot like living in the hood, man. You gotta be in the right gang because they've got your back. Over there, when you're in country, your brothers—I mean, the Corps—they've got your back. Everybody else, they're just trying to stick it to you. I mean, look, man, one day you're trying to help these people build a school or fix a road, and the next day the guy you're helping turns around and blows you up. That's not war, man. That's some kind of royal foul-up. It's just a mess. No way to understand."

"But you decided to be a lifer," Brenden put in. "You went back on a second tour. That's when you got hurt, right?"

"I'm a Marine, man," Carver said. "The Corps is my family.

I already told you that. There's the Corps and Darla, and now there's nothing. I told you all that before."

"I know we've talked about it a little," Brenden said, "but you still haven't told me about the day you got hurt. I mean, how it happened."

Carver sighed. "They're all cowards," he finally said, his tone derisive. "All cowards. I'll tell you something, Doc, I've even seen the tapes. They sit out there a quarter of a mile away with a plunger, waiting for us to drive along in our Humvee with no armor plating. We've just got sandbags up the sides and some old plywood that's supposed to keep us safe. So they sit out there in the desert—a long way away from the road—and when we drive by in caravan, they pick out the vehicle they want in the convoy, and *bang*!"

Brenden waited a beat and then went on. "So tell me the rest of the story, Antwone, if you feel like it."

"So there we were, Doc, in a Humvee. They call it a cardboard coffin—a perfect place to get shredded, you know?" Carver pointed to his shriveling legs and then remembered the doctor's blindness.

"My legs, man. They're shredded."

"Sorry," Brenden said. "I'm so sorry."

Carver went on. "So we're on the road from Fallujah back to Baghdad to Marine Corps barracks. Baghdad. What a waste that is. Six million people sprawled all over the place. Every street, building, and back alley just somewhere else where you can kill a Marine. The whole country's like that. I mean, day after day you drive the highway—the 'Death Highway,' man—from

Fallujah to Najaf, one hundred and fifty miles of death. Day after day, just waiting to be shredded.

"So we're on the road, headed back to Baghdad. There are four of us. We're weapons platoon, you know? Easy company. Fifth Marine Division. And we're proud. Proud of our unit. Proud of our platoon. Proud of the Corps. But ticked off because we're here. So we're out there on patrol looking for the bad guys and just praying not to get shredded. I'm up on top, you know, as a gunner observer. Cassidy's driving. There's a tactile commander, a brother, Lieutenant Brown, and another brother, Jackie Washington, serving as a scout.

"We're driving, and I'm up on top, and I'm vigilant, man. I'm on my game. They call it situational awareness. And I know where I am, man. And I know where I have to be, you see? It's a hundred and twenty degrees out there in the desert, you know? And a hundred and forty inside the Humvee. Air conditioning is a joke. You nearly sweat to death. So I'm studying everything around, and you know what's amazing, Doc?"

"What?" Brenden said.

"The desert sky, man. You know, it's really beautiful. Clear. I mean, unbelievably clear. You can see for miles with the sun reflecting off everything. It's beautiful out there—the colors and everything. Like I said, you can see for miles and miles, but you can't see them. And you can't see the IEDs. That's what they call them, Doc—improvised explosive devices. There's nothing improvised about it, man. It's figured out. They make them out of artillery shells they fill with explosives and bury them under the road. Then *bang*!"

"And that's what happened to you?" Brenden asked quietly.

"*Bang!*" Carver said. "*Bang!* I don't know if I really heard it—the bang, I mean. They say you never hear the one that gets you. I don't know if I actually heard it. The shock picked our Humvee right up in the air. Imagine that, Doc. Over a ton of Humvee just picked up in the air and dropped upside down with me under it. And then the fire and the guys screaming, and I'm shredded. I can't help anyone. And I'm conscious. You know what I mean? I know what's going on, but I can't do anything about it.

"So I hear them all die, man, inside that deathtrap Humvee. Everything's burning. But I'm not inside. The fire's all around, but I'm not in it because I'm the observer. I was on top. They're dead, and I'm alive."

Now Brenden heard the Marine crying, and he sat quietly, letting him go.

"They're dead, and I'm alive! And I'm responsible. I killed them, right along with the Taliban." The young man was sobbing now. "And now I'm here, and I'm worth nothing. And good Marines are dead. And I killed them."

"Listen, Antwone," Brenden said, leaning forward in his chair, "I can't pretend to understand what you're feeling. I mean, I haven't been where you've been, but forty thousand guys have been wounded in this war. Over five thousand Americans are dead. And behind each one of those men there's another American soldier who feels responsible. From what you've described, it wasn't as if you were negligent or you weren't paying attention. What was the phrase you used? You said a Marine has to be situationally aware. Well, from listening to you, it seems to me that you were as aware as a person could be."

"But they're dead!" Carver screamed. "They're dead, and I killed them. I didn't see . . . I didn't warn them . . ." Coming through his sobs, his voice was almost a moan. "I should be dead. I should be the one that's dead."

"I don't think so, Antwone," Brenden said softly. "I think your fellow Marines would want you to live. What do you guys always say? *Semper fi*? Always faithful? Well, I believe you were faithful to your duty, Antwone. Faithful to the Corps and faithful to the three friends you lost. I hear your pain when you tell me you wish it were you that was dead, and I have no doubt that if you could go back in time, you would sacrifice your life for your comrades.

"We've never talked about it, so I don't really know what kind of faith, if any, you have. But in the Bible, Jesus says, 'Greater love hath no man than this, that a man lay down his life for his friends.' I believe that God was speaking directly to you. Your pain is that you *could* not sacrifice—not that you *would* not—and I believe God loves you and knows how much you loved the guys you served with. So the way I see it, both God and I are sure that you've always been faithful. I've already learned how much you love your wife. Whenever you speak of your mother, I know you understand how tough her life has been, and I can hear the softness in your voice when you talk about your brothers and sisters. I know you feel sorry for what has happened to some of them. Remember, Antwone, I told you that I think you're a really good human being who wants to be part of something larger than just yourself. I think you're a team player, and that's a great person to be."

The man had stopped crying and was quiet. Finally he said, "So what do you do when there's no more team? When it's all been taken away?"

"Maybe you find another team," Brenden suggested. "Or maybe you examine the possibility of accepting God as a part of your life. This is not psychiatry, Antwone, but I believe God is always there for you, so you're never really alone. I think maybe you need to find another way of belonging."

He heard Nelson change positions on the floor, reminding him that his canine friend had a story.

"We all struggle to belong," he told the Marine. "Take Nelson here. He started off as a stray puppy living in a state park, eating scraps and drinking from the lake. His trainer adopted him from the SPCA and took him to the guide dog school, where he learned his job. No, he *excelled* as the best guide dog they ever had. Then, he had two different masters. Neither of them worked out. He had . . . too much personality . . . too much energy that the previous masters didn't understand. There he was, with all that training—the best of the best—but useless, with no one to serve, no home, no place to belong. Then I came along, and we fit. I mean, we fit together. We understood each other. The loyalty and love are mutual."

Almost unconsciously, Brenden reached down to touch the dog. He continued, "You never know how it's all going to work out. That's the risk you take putting it out there. You have to keep searching for a place to be yourself and for the people you want to share your life with. I know you believe you found them in the Corps and with Darla. That doesn't mean you can't fit in somewhere else, be valuable, find a place."

Brenden heard the man shrug in his wheelchair. "Yeah, right," he said sarcastically. "There's a place just waiting out there for a no-legged, no-sex black man, right? There's a big place waiting out there in that great big beautiful world just for me. Right?"

"I believe there is," Brenden said, "but why don't we talk about it on Wednesday? I think that's enough for today."

The Marine didn't answer. A moment later, Brenden heard him wheel out of the office.

When Carver left, the doctor sat still, moved to the very core by the intensity of the young man's feelings and by the sense that at this moment, Corporal Antwone Carver, United States Marines, had lost everything. Brenden often empathized with his patients, but his professional responsibility generally allowed him to maintain the objective distance necessary to be truly helpful.

Now, as he sat in his chair, alone with his big dog, he felt an unbelievable level of simpatico for Antwone Carver. *I know what it feels like to be that empty,* he thought, *to feel that worthless, to feel so alone. Somehow I'm going to have to find a way to rebuild Carver's support system, and even more basic, his sense of self-worth. There has to be a button that can be pushed; something that will unlock the pain and lead to healing. Something or someone like Nelson was for me. As a doctor, I have to believe in that truth—and as a person, I've proved it.*

WHEN HE GOT HOME that night, Brenden was even more attentive than usual to his children. And later, when he and Kat went to bed, he felt the need to hold on tight, to keep her close, to value his family and his life more intensely than ever before.

chapter thirteen

Brenden was reviewing his case notes on Antwone Carver, and beyond the obvious pain and loss, Carver's repeated expression of love for his wife continuously shone through. *So why,* Brenden thought, *is Mrs. Carver not here?* Did he have the ethical right to shortcut the arduous process of therapy by talking to her directly? He remembered what "Bad News" Barnes had told him: that sometimes when working with these veterans, you had to "cross the line" and step outside the ethical guidelines of your profession. He was quite sure that if he asked Antwone for permission to talk to his wife, the man wouldn't give it. But surely Mrs. Carver could give needed insight into Antwone's psyche. So what to do?

If Antwone had pushed his wife away, that meant when he

was released from Brenden's care, he would probably return to South Central LA and to what—a life back in the hood with no support and no future? Brenden was not willing to accept that for one of America's finest, and so, breaking every rule, he picked up the phone and called Darla Carver.

"Darla Carver," she answered. The voice Brenden heard sounded intelligent, cool, and careful.

"Mrs. Carver, I'm Dr. Brenden McCarthy. I'm the psychiatrist assigned to evaluate the effects of your husband's injuries up here at Veterans Hospital. I'm sorry I didn't get to meet you while you were here visiting Antwone, but I thought it might be important for us to have a conversation so that I can gain some insight into the direction that I'm taking regarding your husband's therapy."

"I don't want to talk about it," the woman said, surprising Brenden. "Antwone and I will work it all out for ourselves. It's our business. We'll figure it out."

"Mrs. Carver," Brenden said, choosing his words carefully, "I understand the personal nature of what's going on between you and how difficult it must be for you and Antwone to share feelings that are so intimate, but I want you to know that I really care about your husband, and I'm hopeful that the time he and I spend together during treatment can place him on the road to a positive recovery. Please, may I ask you a couple of questions about your relationship with your husband that may shed some important light on the emotions he's expressing?"

There was a pause on the other end of the phone, and Brenden waited.

"Listen, Doctor," she said, "Dr. . . ."

"McCarthy," he prompted. "Brenden McCarthy."

"Well, listen, Dr. McCarthy, I certainly hope you can help Antwone. I've been praying for someone to help him, but I really don't want to talk to you about any of this. It's just too . . ."

Brenden heard her voice break.

"It's too painful. I'm sorry."

"Mrs. Carver," Brenden put in quickly, "please don't hang up. I want you to understand that I have very personal reasons for taking an interest in your husband's case. You see, I am blind, and I lost my sight in an accident—much like Antwone was hurt in war. For both of us, our disability was imposed on us by circumstance rather than by birth. I understand the devastation and trauma that come with a sudden disability like your husband's. Please know that I really want to help him, and talking to you could be invaluable and, I think, make a substantial difference in future adjustment. Would you at least take down my phone number and call me anytime—24/7—if you decide you're willing to talk to me?"

Again there was a pause on the line.

"Okay," she said. "Okay. I'll take your number."

After she had written it down, Brenden said, "I mean it, Mrs. Carver. I really care about Antwone, and I believe there's a lot we can do for him if we work together, so please call me at any time."

After hanging up, Brenden considered what he would do next. He realized that the last session they had shared had been extremely painful for the Marine. Carver was carrying a heavy load of guilt, along with the complete shattering of his self-worth. Brenden felt it was critical to offer Antwone information about options available to paraplegics—both professionally and physically. He would also need to begin clearing up the misinformation that was out there regarding sexual function in spinal cord injury, and so he turned on his computer and began to gather information that he could explain in simple terms to Carver.

He was surprised to find how many Web sites dealt with sexuality in paraplegics with spinal cord injury, and he began to take notes on the material that seemed most cogent to Carver's case.

The first article that caught his attention was written by Irma Fiedler, PhD, associate clinical professor of physical medicine and rehabilitation at the Medical College of Wisconsin.

In a five-year study, she sought to clarify some of the issues surrounding sexuality after spinal cord injury. She indicated that sexual health was not only about function but needed to include an understanding of all the physical and mental sensations of the partners before, during, and after sex. Also, though childbearing could be compromised, McCarthy was delighted to learn that over 80 percent of men suffering spinal cord injury could produce offspring with the support of appropriate medical participation.

On another site he read a significant article written by Dr. Marca L. Sipski. Here the question of the completeness or incompleteness of the patient's injury was raised. Brenden concluded that it all seemed to come down to whether a person's upper or lower neuropaths were affected.

Carver's MRI showed that the young Marine seemed to have maintained some lower motor neuron feeling. This was encouraging, because over 90 percent of the men who had been tested had some kind of erectile function and were able to produce appropriate sperm. From his own academic study, Brenden knew that sexual impulses needed to register in three distinct areas: the sympathetic, parasympathetic, and somatic nervous systems. In the case of Antwone Carver, that information was not yet available, but early indications suggested that the lumbar area of his spine was completely intact; so Carver and his wife should be able to return to a mutually satisfying process of sexual engagement. After all, Carver's libido should be unimpaired. The couple would need a great deal of patience initially, but they would be able to redevelop a close physical relationship.

Brenden sat back in his chair, drumming his fingers on the desk, thankful for the possibilities he would be able to offer Antwone Carver.

DARLA CARVER DIDN'T KNOW how long she had been sitting by the phone. Her mind was in turmoil, trying to decide what to do. On the one hand, she was a very private person, believing that what went on between a husband and wife was not to be shared with anyone. Also, she was a person of deep faith, believing that the power of prayer would lead her to the answers. She was sure that God would point the way if she believed and was open to his Word. But was it possible that this Dr. McCarthy was the instrument God intended? With the blending of his profession as a psychiatrist and the fact that he was blind and had a unique understanding of life with disability, had he been sent to her and Antwone by God? She found herself getting excited at the possibility, and so she reached for the phone.

THE PHONE RANG, JARRING Brenden out of his reverie.

"Hello," he said.

"Dr. McCarthy? This is Darla Carver. Is now a good time to talk?"

Wow, Brenden thought, *my lucky day*. "Sure, Mrs. Carver. Go ahead."

"Please call me Darla," she said.

"Thank you, Darla," he said. "How can I help you?"

"Oh, Doctor," she cried, the dam breaking, allowing her emotions to flow freely. "I just don't know what to do or how to act. Antwone has pushed me away; pushed me out of his life. I just don't know how to handle it. I don't know what to do, what to say. Everything I try to do seems to be wrong."

She was crying now, her voice breaking.

"I mean, I love Antwone, Doctor. I love him so much, but I just don't know how to help him."

"Well," Brenden said, trying to soothe her, "we'll figure that out together, Darla. We're on the same team, you know. We both want Antwone to get healthy, right?"

"Oh yes," she said. "Yes. I just want my husband back."

"Remember I told you I had some questions to ask? Well, here's the most important one. Was there any kind of incident that happened while you were here that may have set him off and precipitated the change in your husband's behavior?"

"I don't know, Doctor. When I arrived and first saw Antwone, I could tell how much it meant to him. I could feel how much he loved me, how much he missed me, how much he needed me. Then after we saw the surgeon, Dr.—what was his name?—Dr. Craig. Yes, that's right, Dr. Craig. After we saw him, everything changed."

"Was there something that this Dr. Craig did?" Brenden asked. "Did he say anything that upset Antwone?"

"I don't know if I should say this," she said quietly, "but he was a horrible doctor. I mean, the way he talked to both of us."

"What do you mean?" Brenden queried, alarmed.

"He was so matter-of-fact, so cold when he talked about Antwone's injury. It was as if he thought being a paraplegic didn't matter. He was just so . . . unemotional."

"I'm sorry, Darla," Brenden said, meaning it. "During my time in practice, I've observed that surgeons tend to function this way. In many cases I think it arises out of their own fears of inadequacy. I believe that many of them think that if they can't automatically fix the problem, they don't want to deal with anything related to adjustment or rehabilitation."

Darla Carver's tone changed abruptly, and Brenden could hear the anger rise in her voice.

"That's not all of it," she said. "When he talked about sex, it was so awful."

"You mean your husband's ability to participate in sex?" Brenden suggested. "You understand, Darla, that there are many ways to deal with this issue, and I'll be happy to point you in the direction of things to read and also talk with both you and Antwone when you come back again."

"Do you think I will?" she asked hopefully. "Do you think Antwone will want me to see him again?"

"I'm sure of it," Brenden said. "Please go on. Tell me more about what this Dr. Craig said."

"Well, he kept looking at me while he was telling Antwone about where his spine was broken and how his ability to have sex would be affected. He just kept looking at me while he . . ." Now she was crying again. "While he took away my husband's manhood!" She paused, and her tears turned to anger. "You know, Dr. McCarthy, I actually think he was hitting on me."

"You what?" Brenden said, shocked.

Darla was even more emphatic. "His eyes never left my body. A woman understands these things. When he shook my hand, his fingers slid up my wrist. And when we sat down, his hand kept brushing my thigh. Then there was the way he gave me a business card with his private number while he was telling my husband that he would be sexually impotent. It was awful! I'm telling you, Dr. McCarthy, he was a pig. A pig! And something should be done about him."

Brenden gripped the phone hard in his right hand, squeezing the receiver, outraged and disgusted.

Working to control himself and remain professional, he said,

"I'll look into all this, Darla, but right now I want you to stay positive and remain hopeful. I think Antwone and I are making good progress, and I don't believe it will be long until you'll be able to come back up here and talk with Antwone yourself."

"You really think so?" she said through her tears. "Do you really think Antwone will want to see me?"

"Remember what I told you," Brenden said. "We'll work on this as a team, Darla. I think Antwone is a great guy, and I can feel how much you love him and how much he loves you. I really appreciate you calling me back, and I'm here to help."

"I know that," she said. "I could hear it in your voice when you talked to me about your own disability. I'm glad you're Antwone's doctor. Please send me any materials I should read and tell me when I can come back to Seattle."

"I promise," Brenden said. "And I promise to have a long talk with Dr. Craig. Oh, one more thing," Brenden said, remembering. "If for any reason you talk to your husband, please don't tell him about our conversation. It could upset him."

"Oh, I understand," Darla said. "I won't say a word. Thank you, Dr. McCarthy."

When they hung up, Brenden went right back to his computer, and this time he was Googling "Dr. Jonathan Craig." Brenden remembered that under full disclosure, all physicians were required to post pertinent information on any malpractice cases in which they were a principal. Upon examination of Craig's file, he knew he had hit the mother lode. Three women had filed separate sexual harassment lawsuits: a nurse and two patients.

What a jerk, Brenden thought. *What a manipulative, miserable person.*

Dr. Jonathan Craig rarely went into the doctors' lounge at the VA hospital. The only time he interacted with his physician colleagues was when consults were necessary or when he needed his morning fix of coffee. It was an addiction, he knew, but he had compensated for it by the treatments he got to whiten his teeth and the Altoids that were always in his pocket just to freshen his breath in case an attractive patient or nurse could not resist his charms.

Women just can't resist, he thought arrogantly. *Except for that black beauty, Darla Carver.* He could have made her so happy, especially considering her husband's impotence. A couple of nights with him would have done her good. *Ah, well, c'est la vie, que sera sera, and all that. Someone else will come around. They always do.*

He saw the tall man and the dog enter the room as he was pouring a second cup. Surgery would be in an hour, and this would be just enough buzz to put him on top of his game.

The blind man had stopped and was speaking to another doctor, who then walked in his direction, with the big dog and the man following easily through the chairs.

"Thank you, Doctor," the blind man said to his friend, who nodded and walked away. "Dr. Craig," Brenden said, "I'm Dr. Brenden McCarthy, the psychiatrist who is treating Antwone Carver, and you're a piece of garbage."

Dr. Craig blinked, nearly dropping his cup as McCarthy stopped directly in front of him. There was an audience now as the heads of all the physicians in the room turned.

"What . . . What are you talking about?" Craig said, trying to gain control of the situation.

"I'm talking about your patient, Antwone Carver. I'm talking about you—not only did you demonstrate incredible insensitivity to his condition, but he could probably bring you up on malpractice charges for hitting on his wife as you were telling him he was going to live the rest of his life sexually shattered. That's what I'm talking about, you low-life scumbag."

Dr. Craig recoiled from the blind man's assault.

"And I'll tell you what else I'm talking about," Brenden went on. "I'm talking about bringing you up on charges to this hospital's medical ethics committee. I'm talking about supporting the Carvers in any lawsuit they might mount and recommending an investigation by the state medical ethics board into your overall patient performance. That's what I'm talking about."

For the first time, Dr. Jonathan Craig felt the veneer that protected his gigantic ego begin to fray.

"Now, Doctor," he said, "I don't think that will be necessary. I'm sure that whatever has gone on with Mr. and Mrs. Carver is nothing more than a simple misunderstanding. I'll call them right away and settle things down."

"You won't call them at all," McCarthy said, moving forward with Nelson, getting right into the guy's face. "You won't disturb them in any way. Let's be clear about that, Dr. Craig. You won't have any contact with them. You're off this case. I'm sure I'm going to gain support for that idea from your chief of staff. I have an appointment with him in an hour."

Now Craig was a little desperate. "Listen," he said, trying to talk to Brenden colleague-to-colleague, "don't you think you're overreacting to the situation a little bit, because of your own . . ." He searched for the words. "Your own circumstance?"

"You mean my disability," Brenden said, his voice resounding in the room with a cutting edge everyone could hear. "My handicap?"

"Well, yes," Craig said, stammering. "Yes. That's what I mean."

"And I suppose you think that Darla Carver was just being overdramatic when she described how you nearly raped her with your eyes. She said it felt like you were taking her clothes off right in front of her husband. Do you think he missed all that, Dr. Craig? Do you think it didn't add to his pain?"

Dr. Craig saw the big dog stiffen and begin to quiver as the blind doctor held the harness in his left hand. Then he heard a low growl coming from deep in the animal's chest.

"You see," Brenden said to the doctor, "my friend Nelson, here, feels exactly the same way I do about your moral conduct. Don't you, boy?"

The growl got loud enough for the whole room to hear, and the dog moved forward a step, causing the doctor to back even farther away.

"Please control your animal," he said.

Brenden smiled. "I wouldn't want him to hurt you the way you've hurt the Carvers. Okay, Nelson," he said, patting the big dog, "I think we have an appointment down the hall with the chief."

Turning, and without another word, the psychiatrist and his guide dog walked out of the lounge, leaving Craig standing alone and embarrassed in front of his colleagues.

chapter fourteen

The rhythm of the session was wrong—very wrong—and Brenden knew it. In therapy, a good psychiatrist may lead in order to draw the patient out, but in general it is hoped that the patient will come to his or her own conclusions. In that way there is a great possibility that the outcome can be lasting.

Wonderful in theory, Brenden thought, but the practical side of his mind said, *He's sending me the wrong messages. There's something not authentic in what he's telling me. Why?*

"Antwone, in one of our early conversations, you were clearly upset when you were talking about sex and Darla. Now you're telling me it doesn't matter?"

"It don't matter, man," Carver said. "I mean, when you ain't got it, you ain't got it. Isn't that right, Doc? Like you, man. You can't see, right? I mean, you're blind, so that's the way it is. And what it is, it is, right?"

"It's not always that black-and-white." Brenden tried to smile. "You know, there is a thing in life called gray, and most of us live in that state most of the time."

"What's that old saying my mother used to tell me? The proof is in the pudding?" Antwone laughed darkly. "Well, there ain't no pop in this pudding."

"Antwone, I'm trying to tell you that's not necessarily true. There have been amazing breakthroughs in spinal cord injury. People can go back to having a very satisfying sex life, even having children."

"Well, that's good for them, Doc, you know. But Darla, she's all woman and needs to be satisfied—the right way, if you know what I mean."

"Antwone, I think you're taking a really limited view on this subject. Look, there are some terrific interviews I'd like you to watch, with couples talking about their sexual relationship after spinal cord injury. I think they're very informative. I've watched them, and they're extremely positive."

"I ain't gonna watch losers have sex, Doc. If I want to see skin flicks, there are better ones on cable. You know what I mean?"

Brenden's mind was spinning, and the question kept pulling on his brain. *Why is this guy being so cavalier about the thing that before meant so much to him? Why is he taking such a different attitude?*

"Have you talked to Darla in the last few days?"

"She's called a couple of times, but I haven't picked it up."

"Why, Antwone? Why haven't you talked to your wife?"

"Because there ain't nothing to talk about, Doc. We're done. I'm done. You know, it's just that simple; it's all over, and it don't matter anymore. It just don't matter."

"Why doesn't it matter?" Brenden pressed. "Why has your attitude about Darla changed?"

"Marvin is right, you know," Carver said. "Sexual healing."

"Marvin?" Brenden asked. "Sexual healing?"

"Marvin Gaye, man. Eighties soul. Weren't you hip back then?"

"I guess not," Brenden said.

"Well, when there's no healing, there's no healing," Carver said, his hands drumming the sides of his chair. "There's no sense trying anymore."

"Antwone, I'd like to suggest that before you give up on your marriage, you have Darla come back up here so that we can all share in this conversation. What do you think?"

"Get out of my face about this," Carver answered angrily. "That just ain't gonna happen. Aren't you listening to me? We're done! I'm done. Can't you just let it go?"

"Antwone, I believe that sometimes when a person is hurt—really deeply hurt—they can become paralyzed by the pain."

Immediately Brenden knew he had used the wrong word.

"That's right," the man screamed. "Finally you got it, man. Paralyzed. Paralyzed. Paralyzed. Nothing works. That's the way it is. That's the way it's gonna be. Nothing working. Period. End of story. We're done."

Abruptly the man's mood shifted, and he began crying. The doctor waited.

In these moments with a patient, it was hard to know what would happen on the other side. Sometimes when the tears stopped, patients would be willing to step back and take another look, but Brenden was sensing that in this case, at the end of the tears, Carver would be even more resigned to the idea that his relationship with his wife—and, Brenden feared, with his life—was finished.

The doctor didn't expect to hear Nelson's chain rattle as the big dog stood, and before he had a chance to command him to lie down again, the animal moved forward toward Carver. Brenden heard the sound of Nelson's nuzzling as he placed his nose in Carver's hand as if to say, *Is something wrong? Can I help?*

Then Brenden heard the rustle of the man's shirt as he pulled his hand away. But the big dog was persistent, and the doctor listened to his paws click on the hospital tile as he moved in even closer, resting his head on the man's knee.

He was about to tell the dog to get back when Carver said, "Good dog. You're a good dog."

The Marine reached forward in his chair, patted the animal, and then Brenden was sure he heard him hug the big dog. *Wow. A new breakthrough—just maybe.*

Nelson stayed still, allowing affection to pass between them.

Brenden remembered the first time he and the dog had shared a moment like this. It was when Smitty, the dog's trainer, and the newly blinded Brenden had gone to the guide dog school to take Nelson out of his kennel in the middle of the night, and for the first time, the animal had chosen to go to Brenden rather than his trainer. Smitty then told Brenden that animals had a special instinct, that they just seemed to know when people really needed them. And as Brenden listened to Carver and the big black Lab, he knew Smitty had been right.

After a while he said, "Antwone, if you can accept love from Nelson right now, isn't it possible that you can find a way to accept love from Darla?"

Carver answered him quietly. "This ain't real love, man. I mean, like between people. This is just a dog. It ain't people."

"But it's real," Brenden said. "Isn't it, Nelson?"

The big dog came back to his master and licked his hand.

"Antwone, after I learned to love Nelson, I was ready to fall in love with my wife—with Kat. Nelson proved that love is an absolute. Everyone wants it. Everyone needs it. Don't close off love because you think someone can't love you back. I don't believe it's only your decision to make. Darla is offering her love to you freely. The question is whether you can accept it in return."

The men were quiet, and Nelson lay down, taking his customary place next to his master. Carver finally broke the silence.

"You just don't get it, do you, Doc?"

"Get what?" Brenden asked.

"Look," Carver said, "when I met Darla, I had the Corps, man. I had—you know—I had big-time game. When you got game, everything's cool."

"Let me ask you something," Brenden said. "When did Magic retire from the Lakers?"

"In '93," Carver said, "when he came down with that AIDS thing."

"Right," Brenden said. "When he contracted AIDS. What do you think when you see Magic now?"

"Oh, man," Carver said, "he's the coolest brother on the block. All the stuff he's done for South Central, with the theaters and Starbucks and all the bling he's given away. Magic's the top brother, man."

"That's right," Brenden said, "and he hasn't touched a basketball in more than a decade. So why do people love Magic so much?"

"Because he's Magic," Carver said. "What are you, stupid? He's Earvin 'Magic' Johnson."

"That's right," Brenden said. "And you're Antwone Jamal Carver."

"Yeah. So?"

"Here's what I think, Antwone. You served your country in a way far greater than Magic served it on a basketball court. You sacrificed for your nation. You're a member of the greatest fighting force on earth—the Marine Corps. And you went to war and fought for us with courage and distinction. I think that's heroic."

"But I came home broken," Carver said, "and now the Corps doesn't want me, and Darla doesn't need me."

"Oh yes, she does," Brenden said.

"How do you know, man?" Carver challenged. "You've never met her. You don't know nothing."

"But I've . . ." Brenden bit his lip, remembering. "But I've heard you talk about her, and it sounds to me that you at least believe she loves you."

"She doesn't love me," Carver said. "She pities me. That's all. Pity isn't love."

"I don't pity you, Antwone," Brenden said. "I admire you."

Carver laughed. "Well, isn't that wonderful? A blind white doctor admires a low-life, no-legged, no-sex black man, right? Isn't that something?"

He laughed again, and Brenden noted the abrupt mood change and decided to probe it.

"So are you feeling sorry for yourself, Corporal?" he asked. "Because that's what I think. I think that instead of stepping up like a Marine, you're copping a plea to pity. Is that what you're doing?"

"Yeah, man," Carver said, agitated. "I feel sorry for myself. You bet I feel sorry. I've been cheated, man. That's the way it is. Cheated by life. I was born with nothing, and I got nothing, and now I'm going to die with nothing. That's the way it is."

"You're wrong, Antwone," Brenden said. "Yeah, you were born in a tough environment, but you did something about it. You joined the Corps, served your country with honor, and married Darla."

"And all that's been taken away," Carver said. "It's all gone."

"You keep saying that," Brenden said. "So, okay, in your head it's gone, but you're here, and tomorrow you have a chance to change it, to try again. Look, I get where you're coming from.

When I went blind, I thought my life was over, but you find out that there's a whole lot more of life to be part of. It's a question of choices. I think you're feeling sorry for yourself and giving up much too early. I think you're quitting. And like you said to me, I think that's stupid. And even more importantly, Antwone, I don't think it has to be like that. I think maybe I'm a good example for you to study."

"Okay," Carver said. "So you're awesome. That's what I'm supposed to think? Dr. Brenden McCarthy, Superman, right, man? Nothing can hurt you—kryptonite, blindness, nothing. Well, a lot of us aren't like that."

"Listen, Antwone," Brenden said, meaning it, "I couldn't do what you did. I would have been scared to death to go to Iraq, to fight there. I think you've got what it takes to do anything, to win at anything. And I think people who are winners are like that from birth. They just have something that makes them special. I believe you're one of those people."

Carver didn't answer, so Brenden pressed the point.

"Antwone, none of this gets solved in a day, or in one session together, or in conversations with Darla, or in rehab, or in going home and starting to look for a new life. It all works one step at a time. That's what we're doing here—working one small step at a time—but I'm telling you, man, some morning you're going to wake up, and it will be like you got to the top of a mountain, and you're looking down on the world, and it looks pretty good down there, and you look back and think, *I made this climb, and now I'm up here.*

"You asked about my life? Well, that's what I did. I did it

literally. Nelson and I went back to the mountain where I got hurt and climbed it together. And we made it. When we were up there together, I thought, *Look at how far we've come.* And that's how I feel today. Sure, there are more mountains to climb, more obstacles in the way, but I believe I can do it, and I know you can do it. It just starts with small steps, so don't quit, Antwone. Don't quit on what's going on here."

As before, the man didn't say anything, and Brenden heard him turn his wheelchair toward the door, dismissing the therapy.

In most cases Dr. McCarthy would stop a patient from cutting off the session—it gave up too much control—but with Carver he had the feeling that he needed to break off their communication so that he could absorb what had happened.

As the Marine turned the doorknob, Brenden asked, "So how are you doing on your meds, Antwone? Is everything going okay? Any reaction that I should be aware of?"

"The drugs? Oh, the drugs. Yeah, they're fine, man. Doing everything they're supposed to do. Can't you tell? I'm feeling good, real good. Can't you see how much better I am?"

The psychiatrist didn't say anything, because another alarm had just gone off in his head.

NIGHT HAD FALLEN, AND Brenden McCarthy couldn't sleep. Slipping out of bed quietly and stepping into his sweats and running shoes, he went downstairs, with the loyal Nelson shaking himself awake and following.

Alone in the dark he poured himself an Irish whiskey and

sat down, holding the glass in both hands and trying to understand what his concern was really about.

The session started badly, but in the end we did pretty well, he thought. *I believe we made some significant progress today. I can't say that Antwone Carver is turning the corner, that he's prepared to take on new direction, but I think we have him thinking about the issues. And that always has to come first.*

"Thank you, Nelson," he said out loud. "I'm starting to believe you're a better psychiatrist than I am. It's about that instinct you've got. It's a lot more perfect than we humans have."

A single thump of the tail said that the animal agreed.

So what is it? Brenden considered again. *Why is my alarm going off? Okay, if it's not something in the session, it has to be an attitude. But about what?*

He snapped his fingers, prompting the dog to lift his head, questioning his master.

"PTSD," he said out loud, "and the drugs. Let's see, how long has he been on the medication? Almost two weeks now, and yet I don't sense its effects when we're together. Why not? I need to check on that tomorrow. I need to talk to Antwone and to the nurses on duty. The drugs clearly should have kicked in by now, and yet he's still manifesting symptomatically the same way he was at the onset of therapy.

"Maybe the dosage isn't correct. I don't think so. The orders were written clearly in terms of the curve he's supposed to follow. So if the dosage is increasing but I'm not seeing the effect during our sessions, what's going on? I'll talk to the nurses and the attending physician tomorrow. Something's weird here. Something's really weird."

Brenden stood and stretched, went to the sink, washed out his glass, and placed the Irish crystal carefully back on the bar.

"Okay, Nelson," he said, "let's go back to bed. Maybe we can get to sleep now. We both could use the rest."

The big dog followed his master quietly up the stairs and into the bedroom. Snuggling in next to Kat and pulling the down comforter up to his neck, Brenden relaxed and tried to settle his breathing. The alarm had stopped ringing in his brain, but his mind was still active with the thought that something must be wrong and that Antwone Carver needed much more attention.

Finally, blessed sleep overtook him, though dawn was only a couple of hours away.

chapter fifteen

Brenden was not the only person losing sleep that night. Marine Corps Corporal Antwone Jamal Carver was wide awake, and he had been that way all night. Over the last hours, he had been taking inventory of his life—the good and the bad; the highs and the lows; love, hate, longing, and loss. He figured that if this was going to be his last night on earth, it was important for him to think about what it had all been worth.

His shaving kit rested on the bedside table, and the pills that he'd been storing rested in the bottom of the case. Three pills a day for twenty-four days; seventy-two slightly soggy little pills that would transport him to—where?

That's interesting, he thought. *Where will I go? Heaven or hell? Or just to nothing?*

He didn't much care. As far as he was concerned, God had let him down anyway. His mother's Jesus had never been interested in him. And besides, he'd just lost his legs in a war in which both nations claimed that God was on their side.

And his neighborhood—where gangs ruled the streets and pimps and drug lords ran the nights—what was God doing about all that? Oh, sure, he had heard the Bible-thumping preachers on Sunday mornings with his mother and had seen the rapture of a choir in full voice, but for him God had never really stepped up, and Antwone Carver had never experienced the power of prayer.

For the thousandth time, the screams of his buddies had surfaced in his mind last night, the intensity so great he felt as though it was happening all over again. He could still hear their dying prayers, asking for God's help to pull them out of the fire after the IED had blown up their vehicle. He could smell their singeing flesh. That memory overshadowed any thought that God would make a difference in his life. So about heaven or hell? It just didn't matter.

He remembered the last time he had talked to his mother. Darla had arranged for her to fly up to see him when he first arrived in Seattle. She had cried and told him that everything would be all right. She said it would be hard for her to cope with the loss of the money that he had been sending her from his combat pay. But she insisted it would all work out and that God would take care of everything. Antwone had hugged her, said good-bye, and believed that she was wrong.

He hoped that she would be okay—that some of his brothers and sisters would fill in the space—but he doubted that. They had enough problems of their own, or they just didn't care.

He speculated on whether Darla would ever get the payoff from his insurance policies. What had that doctor said? He was suffering from PTSD. Maybe that was considered enough of an illness that the insurance companies would pay, and if that happened, Darla could help his mother. They had agreed on that before he went to Iraq, deciding that if anything ever happened to him, Darla would do what she could for his mother.

Things weren't so bad. There were some loose ends he couldn't do much about, but it seemed to Antwone that except for Darla, life would go on pretty well without him.

But then there was Darla—his Darla—the only person he truly loved. Involuntarily he started to cry, and for a while he was overcome by sadness. He didn't want to leave Darla, but he was sure that it was the best thing for him to do. All of Dr. McCarthy's talk about a good future just wasn't real. What did the doc know about not being able to feel anything below the waist? Nothing. Nothing at all.

Anyway, Darla was young. She would find someone else. The brothers would line up for her. He had no doubt that was the way it would be. All at once he was overwhelmed by the desire to hear her voice one more time, to hold on to the sound of it, to have just one more memory of his beautiful wife before crossing over.

He didn't want to alarm her, but he decided that even at this hour he had to make the call.

"Hello," she said in that husky-sleepy way he loved when he used to wake up at night and talk to her. "Hello," she said again.

"I love you, Darla," he said.

"Antwone," she said, instantly awake. "Antwone, I love you. Are you okay? Is something wrong?"

"No," he said. "No, everything's fine, girl. I just couldn't sleep, and, you know, I just needed to hear your voice."

"I'm glad," she said. "I'm so glad. I love you, Antwone. Are you calling to tell me you want me to come back up there?"

Now the words were tumbling out of her.

"I can leave school, get on a plane, be there tomorrow. Is that what you want, Antwone? Because that's what I want. I miss you. I love you. I want to be with you."

Carver choked back tears as he heard his wife's pleading, offering herself, offering her love.

"I'm not ready for that, Darla," he managed to say. "I'm just not ready yet."

"But you're calling me," she said. "That tells me you miss me and love me."

Now he couldn't stop the tears.

"You're my whole world," he said. "You're everything, Darla. You know that. You know how much I love you."

"So let me come up there, Antwone. Let me come right now."

"Not now, Darla. Like I said, I can't handle it yet."

"Listen to me, Antwone," she said. "I've been reading about couples who live with your kind of spinal injury. I've been reading that they can love each other, but listen to me. It doesn't even matter about the sex. Our relationship is not just about sex, Antwone; we're about love—our love. I just want to be with you, don't you see? I need to be with you. I need you. Why can't you see that, Antwone? Why do you keep pushing me away?"

Antwone didn't answer because he didn't know the answer. All he felt at the moment was utter, total sadness. He was—what? He thought about it. He was empty, without the capacity to love, even though his wife was offering him so much.

"Darla," he said, struggling to get the words out, "you know how much I love you. You're the only good thing that ever happened to me, Darla; you and the Corps. I hope I've made you happy sometimes. I hope you don't feel like you've wasted your life loving me."

"Antwone, you're my husband. *You're* the best thing that ever happened to *me*. When we're together I'm a whole person, and when we're apart I'm just Darla. I learned that when you were over there. Oh, sure, I'm a teacher. I love the children I teach. I love my family. But when you're not here, I'm not complete. Do you understand that, Antwone?"

"I just hope you've been happy, Darla," he said. "I always want you to be happy."

"I'll get a plane ticket tomorrow," she pressed. "I'll be there with you."

He could feel himself choking again on his tears. All he could say was, "We'll see, Darla. We'll see."

"Oh, Antwone," she said. "I'm so glad you called. I love you so much."

"You, too, Darla. I'll love you forever."

He pushed the button, ending the call, and reached for the case on his bedside table.

SURPRISINGLY, BRENDEN WAS AWAKE. As far as the black dog was concerned, he and his master had just gone back to sleep, but here they were already, heading downstairs to start the morning coffee. In the kitchen, on impulse—or was it something more?—he picked up the phone and dialed veterans hospital, asking the operator for the nurses' station on five.

"Nurses' station. Jamee Edwards speaking."

Brenden knew the voice.

"Oh, Jamee," he said, "it's Dr. McCarthy. Good morning."

"Good morning, Doctor. You're up early."

"I know. I couldn't sleep. Hey, Jamee, would you do me a favor?"

"Sure. What's that?"

"Would you go down and check on Antwone Carver, please? We had a rough session yesterday, and I just want to know he's okay."

"I understand, Dr. McCarthy. Would you like me to call you back?"

"No, that's not necessary, Jamee. Just be sure that everything's all right with him, would you? Thanks a lot."

Brenden hung up just as Kat came into the kitchen.

"What's going on?" she asked. "I heard you talking to another woman."

Brenden could tell she was smiling.

"Caught again," he said. "Can't a guy get away with having an affair in this day and age?"

"Not you," Kat teased. "You can't get away with anything. So what was the call about?"

"Oh, I've been worried about Antwone Carver. You remember, the Marine with major spinal cord injury and PTSD that I've been treating? I just haven't been able to reach him, Kat, and, well, I'm worried."

"The little voice?" she said. "The one you've always trusted?"

"The very same one that told me I should marry you, dear."

"Ah," she said, putting her arms around him. "The best decision you ever made."

NURSE JAMEE EDWARDS WAS married to a career officer in the Navy, and the military had been part of her life for generations. Her father and brothers were all military, and she cared for every one of these guys with a passion built on love and respect.

As always, she knocked on the closed door and waited for a response.

Not unusual, she thought. *It's still pretty early.*

Following protocol, she opened the door and announced herself.

"Good morning, Corporal Carver. It's Jamee Edwards."

Entering the room, she saw Antwone lying on his back, his face peaceful in . . . *Oh no!* Before she could think "sleep," she heard his shallow breathing and rushed to the side of the bed. Grabbing his limp wrist, she took his pulse—faint and rapid. Reaching across the bed, she pulled the alarm for code blue and then raced for the door. Within a few seconds, feet came pounding down the hall as professionals gathered, working to save the life of Marine Corporal Antwone Carver.

chapter sixteen

Brenden felt a queasy concern rising in his chest when the telephone rang just ten minutes after he had talked to the nurse about Antwone Carver.

"Dr. McCarthy, it's Jamee. We have a problem here. Corporal Carver . . ." She paused. "I believe Corporal Carver tried to commit suicide."

"Oh no!" Brenden said, not hiding his emotion. "I'll be there as quickly as I can, Jamee. What are they doing to him now?"

"They've stabilized him, and now they're beginning to intubate him. We're fortunate that he's young and strong. The emergency team feels they can pull him through."

"Let's hope so," Brenden said. "I'll be there as soon as I can."

Brenden hung up and didn't even bother to change into his work clothes. He picked up Nelson's harness and leash and headed out the door, still in his workout gear, to take an earlier ferry.

HIS MIND WAS CHURNING—aching with thoughts of personal failure. He had failed Antwone Carver. He had pushed too hard. He wasn't prepared to take on the problems of a veteran. He expected these guys to be able to cope with their disabilities the way he had. He wasn't empathetic enough. He hadn't wanted to be involved in the first place. Why had he not followed his own instincts? And now his patient was lying in bed, alive but broken, because he had failed. The blind doctor had been too blind to see the effect his personal agenda had imposed on Corporal Antwone Carver. The bottom line—he was completely to blame, and he would have to live with that the rest of his life, both as a professional and as a man.

Arriving at the hospital, he and Nelson went straight to the fifth floor. Brenden was relieved to hear that Carver was conscious, though groggy and heavily medicated. The nurse in the room told him that Carver was under suicide watch, which Brenden knew meant he had restraints on his arms and an IV drip pumping fluids into him.

Brenden found a chair near the head of the man's bed, tied Nelson's leash to the chair leg, sat down, and waited. If Carver saw him, he chose not to acknowledge the doctor's presence, so Brenden just sat quietly, waiting, prepared to stay there as long as it took for the Marine to speak to him.

Clinically, Brenden understood that it was critical for him to find just the right beat—the right note of communication—when Carver first spoke. The man had to know that Brenden was in his corner and wasn't in any way blaming him for trying to take his own life. Forging a bond of trust at a moment like this could go a long way, Brenden knew, toward giving the Marine back his life. And so he waited.

Eventually Antwone spoke in a whisper, forcing even Brenden, so sensitive to sound, to put his head close to his mouth in order to hear.

"Why didn't you just let me die?" the man croaked. "Why didn't you let me take the coward's way out? That's all I deserve."

Brenden took a deep breath. "We didn't let you go, Antwone, because the people who love you think you have a lot to live for, and we know our lives are better off with you in them. That's how I feel. And most importantly, I know that's how your wife feels."

"You talked to Darla?" the man croaked. "You told her?"

"Yes, I did, Antwone. I told her you had an incident."

"An incident?" the man said, his voice a little louder. "I tried to kill myself, man. That's not an 'incident.'"

"I told her we would be able to stabilize you physically over the next couple of days."

"Is she coming up here?" Carver asked, angry.

"No. Not now," Brenden said. "I felt that had to be your decision, so I asked her to remain in San Diego. At least for now."

"Thanks," Carver mumbled.

"Listen, Antwone," Brenden said, "when you got hurt in Iraq, even though you were—what's that word you guys use?—*shredded*, you made it. And now it looks like you're going to make it again. The point is, it doesn't seem like it's your time. I think you have a lot to do in this life, and I want to help you get on the path to doing all those things. After you've rested for a couple of days, let's talk about it, okay?"

No sound came from the man in the bed, so Brenden tried again.

"Antwone, there's something I want to tell you—if you're up to listening to me."

"I got nowhere to go, man," Carver said. "My legs don't work, and I'm tied to the bed, so there's nowhere to go."

Brenden turned to Jamee, the nurse he had spoken to after Carver first attempted suicide. "I need a few minutes alone with Corporal Carver. As his psychiatrist, I'll take complete responsibility for being here alone with him, okay?"

"I don't know, Doctor. Given the current protocol, I don't know if I'm allowed to—"

"I said I'll take complete responsibility. I just need a few minutes. Ten minutes, tops," Brenden told her.

"All right, Doctor," she said, still hesitating. "I'll be back in ten."

Brenden turned back to the man in the bed. "Antwone, do you remember I told you about how I went blind? About the fall I had on a mountain?"

Brenden heard the pillowcase crinkle as the man nodded his head.

"Well, when I woke up and found out I was blind, I figured that was the end of the line. I didn't want to live anymore because there was nothing to live for. Back then I had a girl. Her name was Lindsey. And the truth was . . . Well, the truth was, she couldn't handle my blindness. As far as she was concerned, my disability got in the way of her life plan, and so our relationship ended."

"See, man, that's what I'm telling you," Carver said.

Brenden interrupted. "That will not be Darla, Antwone. She loves you. We'll talk more about that in a while. But for now, let me tell you a little more of my story.

"So I went home, and for a long time I just stayed in my room, feeling really sorry for myself. Eventually my mother talked me into going to rehab and then to the guide dog school, where I got Nelson."

"He's a good dog," Carver said, looking at Nelson lying on the floor next to his master. "He's really a good dog. I never liked dogs, you know, but Nelson, he's special."

"That's right," Brenden agreed. "He's special because he loves me. There's a lot to be said for love, Antwone. A lot to be understood about the power of love. It forges a loyal and unbreakable bond between two people—or between a man and his dog."

"So anyway, I went to the guide dog school and got Nelson, but when I got home, that's when Lindsey—the girl I was in love with—that's when Lindsey quit on the relationship. It was pretty tough when it happened. I went to her apartment and found her with another guy."

Carver whistled between his teeth. "That's hard, man," he said. "That's really hard. So what did you do?"

"Well, I went out and got loaded. I mean, really drunk. And then I wandered around with Nelson in the middle of the night, until I came to a street without any traffic—at least not at that moment. I walked right out into the middle and just sat down."

"You what?" Carver said. "You sat down in the middle of the street? Why?"

"What do you think?" Brenden asked.

"Really?" Carver said. "You too? You wanted to end it?"

"I wanted a car to come around the corner and do it for me," Brenden said. "Life had no meaning. I had no meaning. I just wanted it over with."

"What happened? How come you're still here?"

"Because of Nelson," Brenden responded. "He wouldn't let me stay there in the street. He kept pulling on my arm, trying to pull me to the sidewalk. Eventually he got so aggressive that he bit through my clothes and made my arm bleed. Then he laid down beside me. I tried to command him to leave, I pushed him away, but he wouldn't budge. I got the message. Nelson wasn't about to let me die. He loved me too much to let me go. He would die with me before he'd leave me. His willingness to sacrifice for me changed my attitude."

And now Brenden took a real chance.

"Antwone," he said, "that's the way Darla is thinking. She loves you. She can't let you go. If you end it, you end life for her. Oh, sure, she'll keep living, but she'll never be the same person,

I promise you. She'll never be the same, and I know you would never do anything to hurt your wife. You're too good for that."

Brenden could hear the Marine crying.

"I mean it, Antwone. I know you're too fine a person and love Darla too much to do anything that would hurt her."

"What are you, crazy, man?" Carver said, still crying. "She's my life. Darla's my heart. Darla's everything."

"I know that, Antwone," Brenden said. "I know that. And so we have to work together to make sure that Darla never, ever gets hurt—and to make sure that you two can have a life together."

In a small voice, the Marine said, "You really think that Darla and I can have a life, Dr. McCarthy?"

"Yes, I do," Brenden said. "I believe you and Darla can have love and life, a satisfying marriage, and maybe even children. I think all of that is possible, but we have to begin putting the pieces back together. So you just rest for a couple of days, and then we'll take a fresh look at it, okay?"

"Okay," the Marine said shakily. "Okay."

As Brenden moved toward the door, guided by Nelson, Carver stopped him.

"Hey, Dr. McCarthy?"

Brenden turned. "Yes, Antwone?"

"Doc, remember I told you in the Corps, we have a thing called an 'Alive Day'?"

"Alive Day," Brenden said. "Yes, I remember."

Carver went on, "Well, it's when you've been hurt—you know, in combat—but you've made it; it's the day you know that you're alive. Here's the thing, Doc. Maybe I've had two Alive Days: one over there and one today. Maybe I have to think about doing something with that kind of luck. You know what I mean?"

Brenden nodded, turned, and left the Marine alone to think about it.

chapter seventeen

Over the next three days, Brenden wondered what state of mind he would encounter when he and Antwone Carver had their next session. He was encouraged to hear from the on-duty nurses that Carver was taking his meds, and this time he wasn't trying to hide the pills.

That's a positive, Brenden thought. But medications were only part of a life picture. Would Carver be able to navigate the complications of his disability? Would he be able to accept a renewed relationship with his wife? Could he ever get over the self-pity and self-loathing that were such a struggle for many disabled people?

As Brenden waited with Nelson for the Marine to roll into the office, he found his own anxiety level was surprisingly high.

So he sat in his office chair, working to slow his breathing and gather his thoughts for the session.

This would be a day, he felt, that he would be leading Carver. He knew about the pitfalls of disability. He knew about many of the options for newly injured vets, and more importantly, he knew how critical it was to turn desolation and isolation into engagement and participation with the world at large.

Nelson heard Carver's arrival outside the door before Brenden did, and as the man wheeled in, the big dog was right there to greet him. There was no hesitation on Carver's part to share affection with the big animal. Brenden filed that fact away under the category "hopeful."

"How are you, Antwone?" Brenden asked. "Are you feeling better?"

"I guess so," the man said, embarrassed. "Yeah, I'm feeling better. I'm taking my meds now."

"Yes, the nurses told me," Brenden said, not wanting to give the impression that he was checking up on the Marine.

"I don't really know what good a bunch of pills will do," Carver said.

"Remember what I told you the other day? It's one step at a time. You know, getting to the top of the mountain and then looking down on the world below and thinking, *Wow, I really made this climb!* Antwone, today I want to talk to you about possibilities, things you can look forward to when you get out of this place."

Carver sounded that one-note laugh of disgust that Brenden had heard before.

"Yeah," he said, "and I've got a bridge you can buy cheap."

Brenden chose not to acknowledge the shot.

"I want to talk about what the law provides, what your service to your country guarantees, and what you can expect out there when you deal with the public."

"Oh, you mean when they pity me or think I'm a freak?"

"I don't think that's being fair to people, Antwone," Brenden said. "A lot of us think you're a hero."

"But you still pity me, right?"

"No. That's not how I feel about you," Brenden told him.

"Well, you're a freak too," Carver said. "It sucks, man. I mean, I avoided the gangs in the hood, and now I'm in a big gang, a gang of losers."

"There's power in that," Brenden suggested. "A lot more power than you might expect. Have you ever heard of the Americans with Disabilities Act?"

"Why would I know about that?" Carver asked.

"The Americans with Disabilities Act," Brenden explained, "provides all kinds of support for those of us with disabilities. It guarantees that we cannot be discriminated against because of our disability when it comes to jobs or housing. Along with the ADA, there's something called the Individuals with Disabilities Education Act, which provides every child and adult coping with disability the chance to gain an equal and appropriate education under the law. This all connects to your rights as a GI. Remember, as a Marine, the GI bill is still in place, so you can pursue any field of interest and have it funded, Antwone. That's a lot better than most people have."

"You know, Doc," Carver said, "you don't know much about anything. I'm still black, and now I'm disabled. That's two strikes, and then there's sex. Looks to me like that's strike three. I'm out."

"Wait a minute," Brenden said, turning his face directly toward the Marine. "There are too many people in the world using their labels as an excuse to feel sorry for themselves. You're black. I'm blind. He's gay. She's divorced. We could go on and on, applying our stereotypes to get out of taking responsibility for our actions. Here's the real secret, Antwone. When we apply a label that limits us, the only person who pays the price is us. If you live life on the sidelines and refuse to play the game, the only loser is you."

"Thanks for the halftime speech, Coach," Carver said, "but you're not black, and you're not in this chair."

"And you're not blind," Brenden told him. "I'm not trying to tell you I understand all of the things you're feeling, but I do know it's important to not allow your disability to dominate your potential to find your ability. There's a whole lot you can do, Antwone. A whole lot of things you can be. But it's all on you."

"That's right," the Marine said, getting angry. "That's right. It's all up to me."

"Antwone, there's another part of the secret I want you to learn," Brenden said. "I believe that you can turn being black and being in a wheelchair and coming from a rough background from disadvantages to advantages. I told you about some of the laws surrounding disability, and you know about stuff like affirmative action and racial profiling. The point is, anything we view as a negative can be turned into a positive if you want it enough.

"Take my blindness, for example. I mean, being blind has some amazing advantages. I'll tell you something. I've never met an ugly person, unless they wanted to be. And I've enjoyed a world of senses—smell and touch and taste and sound—that most people never take the time to appreciate. I was telling my kids about that just the other day.

"I know my wife, Kat, is a beautiful woman, but that's not why I love her. I love her because she's beautiful inside. And my children, I think they've benefited because I'm blind. I'm looking forward to you meeting them because they're really sensitive kids, and they don't have any built-in prejudices when it comes to getting to know someone."

"Doc, let me give you a piece of therapy," Carver said. "You're crazy, jack. You're trying to tell me that to grow up the way I did—a brother in a bad neighborhood—can make being black cool? And you're trying to tell me that being in this wheelchair, paralyzed—I can turn that into an advantage? That's a sham, man."

Brenden didn't back off.

"That's exactly what I'm saying, Antwone, but it starts with your developing an attitude that opens up all of the possibilities."

"Attitude schmatitude," Carver said. "When I was in school, that's what they used to tell me. 'Antwone,' the teacher would say, 'you have a bad attitude.' And she was right, and it was my attitude that made me a great Marine."

"Okay," Brenden said. "Then apply that same kind of attitude to becoming successful back out in the world. Redirect all of that nerve and grit into your current situation. Learn your rights and use your talents to get ahead. When you get out of here, I think it would be great if you'd spend some time with a good career counselor, and, Antwone, you'll have time. You'll be on disability for your injuries, so there'll be some dough coming in.

"One of the wonderful things that's happened recently under the law is that you're allowed to pursue a career without losing any of your health benefits. It's taken a lot of years to get that legislation through Congress, but now guys in your situation can feel they're protected while they work to develop a new life. Look, I'm not trying to tell you that it's easy out there, but what I am trying to say is that there is tremendous potential and that you can be hopeful about the possibility of creating a terrific future."

Carver was quiet, thinking.

After a minute, he asked, "How did you develop this attitude, Doc? I mean, how did you get this positive act of yours together?"

Brenden smiled. "A really special guy put me straight. His name is Marvin Barnes. He's a brother, and his story is a lot like yours. He was in Vietnam and got shredded and had some good reasons to feel sorry for himself. He had been the number one draft choice for the Denver Broncos; a three-hundred-pound defensive tackle with the whole world at his feet. But he got drafted and went to Vietnam."

"That's tough, man," Carver said.

"You bet," Brenden said. "Oh, and I forgot to mention he went blind from a war injury."

"Blind?" Carver said.

"You bet," Brenden told him. "My friend went blind, and so everything was messed up for him. No more football. No more life. But he pulled himself together. He's married with a great family, and he does the same kind of work I do. He was my counselor, just like I'm your doctor now."

"And he really has a good life?" Carver asked, becoming interested.

"He has a great life," Brenden said. "He's married, has three kids, lives in a nice house in Colorado. And if he were here now, he would be telling you the same things I am. In fact, a lot of this conversation is just like one I had with him years ago."

"But your friend, I mean, the brother, what about sex?" Carver asked. "You said he has children."

"That's right. He wasn't affected in that way, Antwone, but like I told you, over 80 percent of the guys who have suffered spinal cord injury and are paras have gone on to have very satisfying sex lives and even families."

Brenden paused to let that sink in. "It comes down to this, Antwone. Sex might not be the same as it used to be between you and Darla, but that doesn't mean it can't be satisfying. So does having this conversation mean you're considering letting Darla come to Seattle so you can spend some time together?"

"I'm thinking about it," Carver said. "I don't know, man. I just don't know yet."

"That's all right," Brenden said. "Take your time, but I think you're headed in the right direction. Remember, a few days ago you were as low as it gets. Time is on your side, Antwone."

"I know," Carver said. "You keep telling me one step at a time, or maybe it's one wheel at a time."

Brenden smiled and clapped his hands. "Now, that's a big step. When you learn to joke about your disability, it means you're starting to think about it in a positive way. You're beginning to find balance."

"I don't know," Carver said. "I still feel real shaky, Doc."

"Let me tell you something, Antwone," Brenden said. "I've been blind now for a few years, and there are still some times when I feel sorry for myself and feel—how did you put it?—shaky. Nobody's that secure. Everybody has doubts and fears. Everyone wonders if they can get their stuff together. But in a way, it's our insecurity that creates our drive to become secure. That's part of how we grow. You know who Bill Russell was, don't you?"

"Sure, man. The old dude who played for the Celtics way back?"

"That's right," Brenden said. "The old dude with eleven championship rings."

"Eleven?" Antwone said, amazed.

"That's right. Bill Russell has eleven championship rings, and every night they played, before the game would start, the team would have to wait in the locker room while the big fella threw up."

"He puked?" Carver said, almost laughing.

"You bet. He threw up before every game because he was nervous about how he would play. You get it, Antwone? Nobody's that secure. We're all a little scared. Hey, listen," Brenden went on, "I've been thinking. I bet you could use a little R & R out of this place. You're probably going a little stir-crazy."

"What do you mean?" Carver asked. "Aren't you all watching me in case I decide to take the pipe again?"

"Antwone," Brenden said seriously, "I don't think that will ever happen again. I think you've got too much to live for, and I think you know that."

The man's silence was a tacit admission, as far as Brenden was concerned.

"So anyway, I've arranged with the hospital for you and me to take a road trip."

"Where are we going?" Carver asked.

"That," Brenden said, smiling, "is a secret, but I think you'll like it."

Brenden took control of the close of their session. "That will be all for today, Antwone. I think we've covered a lot of ground, and I hope you feel you got something out of our conversation."

"Yeah," the man said. "It was okay talking to you today, Doc. Okay."

Brenden stood and opened the door, and he heard Carver reach out to pat Nelson good-bye as he wheeled past him.

AFTER THE MAN HAD left, Brenden picked up the phone and called Kat.

"Hey, Kat," he said. "Can you get a sitter for tonight?"

"Probably," she said. "What do you have in mind, big fella?"

"I was thinking dinner in town and a couple of drinks with my best girl. Today was a good day, Kat. I think I'm beginning to break through with Carver, and it feels good. It didn't start off that way, but now it feels real good."

"Okay," she said. "I'll dress up just for you."

"You're beautiful all the time," Brenden said, meaning it. "Dressed or undressed."

chapter eighteen

Two nights later, Brenden and Kat borrowed a hospital van with a hydraulic lift that could easily handle Antwone Carver's wheelchair. At this point in his therapy, he had not yet been fitted for an updated chair, and he was still a little awkward as he worked to maneuver his antique clunker.

Brenden had gone online and learned a lot about the NWBA—the National Wheelchair Basketball Association. And, frankly, he was amazed. There were teams from all over the country, with regional and national championships held in the tournament model of the NCAA. Also, every competitor who participated seemed to be driven, wanting to make it all the way to the Paralympic Games—the Olympics for disabled athletes.

Tonight they would be going to a local high school gym to watch the Seattle High Rollers take on a team from San Jose, California, called the California Gold.

Kat was amazing, Brenden observed, as she drove them to the gym while carrying on an animated conversation with Antwone Carver. Brenden was grateful for how gifted his wife truly was. As he listened, he couldn't help but notice how Kat was able to pull things out of Carver much more easily than he did during their sessions. He thought it was incredibly charming that Carver called her "ma'am" and that there was no street language coming from the Marine in their interaction. Carver, Brenden realized, was quite a gentleman, and that must have been part of what Darla had seen in him during their courtship.

Kat got him talking about his mother and his life in South Central LA. She asked him about who had influenced his life and whether he still stayed in contact with some of them. She gently guided the conversation as Carver described how sad he was about what had happened to some of his brothers and sisters and how much he wished that he'd had a father figure in his life.

Kat made an easy transition, almost seamless, to the subject of whether Carver himself wanted children.

When Brenden overheard this interaction, he at first worried that his wife had forgotten about the man's sexual issue, but as he continued listening, he realized that she was putting a human face on the problem—allowing for perspective. *Incredible,* he thought. *Wow, what a woman! And what terrific instincts she has. Maybe instead of a teacher, Kat ought to consider becoming a therapist.*

As they pulled up to the gym, Carver asked, "So, Doc, what are we doing here?"

"We're gonna see some hoop, my man," Brenden said. "Some big-time B-ball played by some remarkable people."

The sign out front advertising the game said Rollers Rule—Gold Rush Stops Here.

After getting Carver out of the van, they entered the gym to find a good crowd gathered—maybe a couple thousand, Brenden judged by the sound. But right away, Carver stiffened.

"This isn't cool, Doc," he said. "I don't want to watch cripples play the game. It's stupid, man. This is basketball."

"Yes, it is," Brenden said, "and I think you're going to be amazed, Antwone. These are real athletes, you know. And just like you, they had to find another way to play the game they love. Look, just check it out, okay? If you don't like it after the first half, we'll go home. All right?"

"Come on, Antwone," Kat added. "I have a sitter for the night. This game got me out of the house. Let's at least try it for a while."

Carver hesitated for a second, then said, "Okay, we'll take a look."

As the team lined up for the tip-off, Brenden said, "There are a lot of similarities between this game and the NBA. First of all, they play four quarters, twelve minutes each. They have a twenty-four-second rule on the shot clock, like the pros. And the eight-second rule on getting it across half court is the same. Traveling is defined when a guy has pushed his chair twice—just like taking steps before he dribbles—and if he makes an extra push, that's traveling, just like walking in the NBA.

"Fouls are similar, but in this game they call them physical advantage fouls. For example, if a guy's going to take a shot, the defensive man can't wave his hands in front of the guy, blocking his vision. That's considered taking physical advantage. You see a lot of holding fouls, along with charging and blocking.

"And they make a big deal out of making sure all the wheelchairs are uniform in specs. For example, everybody's seat rails cannot exceed eighteen inches from the court's surface, and there can be no extensions for footrests or casters that keep the chairs from tipping over that extend beyond the wheels."

Within five minutes of the start of the game, Antwone Carver, despite himself, was very interested. He couldn't believe the dexterity of the players and how well they passed and shot the ball. At one point he hit Brenden in the ribs.

"Hey Doc, you should have seen the screen this guy set. There was some pretty fierce physical contact."

"Oh, I heard it," Brenden said. "Those wheels may be rubber, but I heard the chairs come together. And check out the way that one chair guy got rocked on the pick. I'm amazed the ref missed it, because I sure heard it. And how about the sweet shot by the open guy? Nothing but net. Swish from twenty feet."

Brenden went on enthusiastically. "You know what I love? The smell of a gym when real athletes are playing. This smells like a gym, doesn't it? All the tension. This place is loaded with testosterone, enthusiasm, and athleticism. I just love being here. So what do you think, Antwone? Do you think it's real basketball now?"

"Okay, okay," Carver said, almost smiling. "It's cool, Doc; it's cool."

Brenden could tell the Marine's eyes never left the court, so he stopped the sales pitch and let the man just watch.

In the third quarter two guys got into a pushing match along the baseline, and the referee had to step in to stop a fight.

"These guys really mean business, man," Carver said to Kat. "I mean, that one dude really wanted to get it on with the Roller guy. Heavy, man. It's really heavy."

In the fourth quarter the star player from the Rollers—number twenty-one—fouled out with his sixth personal. The last call was disputed as to whether it should have been called charge or block, but the referee was clear, and the Rollers were down their best player.

Brenden explained to Carver, "In wheelchair basketball, there are three classes of players based on the nature of their disability. For example, Antwone, because you have complete use of your upper body, you would be a class 3A player and count for three points if you were on the court for your team. No team can have more than twelve points represented on the floor at any one time.

"So with the loss of their star player, the Rollers have decided to play with only four men for the rest of the game, rather than bring in someone off their bench whose disability is more involved. That's the coach's decision. We'll have to see if it works out."

Throughout the night, Kat was giving Brenden a play-by-play and doing a pretty good job. He remembered she had played basketball in high school, and her commentary wasn't bad.

At the end of regulation, the score was 58–58, requiring that the teams play a five-minute overtime. With a thrilling last-second shot, the Rollers won 68–65 when a woman—that's right, a woman—hit a three-pointer to seal the victory.

The gym erupted, and the Rollers paraded around the court with the crowd chanting, "Rollers rule! Rollers rule! Rollers rule!"

Even Carver got swept up in the excitement, and though he didn't join in the chanting, Kat told Brenden that the man was smiling with appreciation and respect. Following the celebration, Brenden introduced himself, along with Carver and Kat, to the Rollers coach—a thirty-eight-year-old quadriplegic who couldn't play but had found his calling as a recruiter and teacher. His name was Barney Rothstein, and he was a quad because of a gymnastics accident fifteen years earlier.

Brenden could imagine the look of astonishment on Carver's face as he learned that Barney had a wife and three children, and that besides coaching, the man had a job as an accounting vice president at Ernst & Young, a major firm in downtown Seattle.

Barney sized up Carver right away.

"You have the look of a guy who played some major hoop before you got hurt, right?"

"I played a little," Antwone said, still guarding his emotions. "Yeah, I played some ball."

"So what did you think of our game?" the coach asked. "What a minute," he added. "Let's talk about that after we've had a couple of beers. What do you say? Look, all of us are going around the corner to a neighborhood pub called O'Malley's. When we roll in there, we take over the joint."

And fifteen minutes later, Brenden, Kat, and Carver understood why. Twelve people in wheelchairs, along with a retinue of friends and family, caused quite a stir when they wheeled into the crowded pub, and Barney, the most disabled of the group, had no problem getting the waitstaff to pull tables together and clear space.

"Get us some shots all around," he cried to the barkeep. "We are the Rollers—and after this win tonight, we're the High Rollers."

"Yeah," they all said in unison. "High Rollers rule! High Rollers rule!"

The chant went on, with beer mugs pounding out the rhythm on the wooden tables.

The cacophony is wonderful, Brenden thought. *What an example of disability turned into ability.*

Somewhere during the second round of toasts and fellowship,

Barney slid his electric chair up next to Carver. Brenden couldn't hear what they were saying, but he hoped the coach was denting the Marine's defensive shell.

"So," Barney said to Carver, "I started to ask you before. What did you think of the game?"

"It was okay," Antwone said. "Yeah, it was all right."

"Okay?" the coach said. "We were awesome tonight, man. Did you see how our guys moved the ball? And how about the three-pointer that Erica hit to win it? I think we were a little better than okay. You know the only difference between our game and the one that you play on two legs?"

"What do you mean, man?" Carver asked. "The only difference?"

"Yeah," Barney said. "The only difference is that they play a vertical game, and our game is horizontal."

"What are you talking about?" Carver asked.

"Well, we don't jump," Barney said. "I mean, that's obvious. But we move the ball with the same kind of precision, and we play defense the same way. I mean, you saw it tonight. Sometimes we were in a man-to-man; sometimes we played zone. And if you think it's not a workout out there, wait until you try it. The cardiovascular stuff going on when you're moving the chairs . . . you're exhausted, man. Did you see how often I had to substitute? Nobody could play forty-eight. Guys are dying out there. You've got to keep your lineup fresh. That's why we have at least ten players dressed for every game.

"Take a look at these people, Antwone," Barney went on. "They're husbands, fathers, and wives. Most of them have jobs, and they're all working to have a better life. The game is what makes them feel good about themselves. Hey, let me ask you something. When you were back in your neighborhood, and you played on the playgrounds or on your high-school team, isn't that what the game meant to you? It made you feel good about yourself?"

Carver shrugged. "It was everything," he said quietly. "The game was everything. It was going to be my way out of the hood. It was how a short guy felt tall. It was the thing that gave me the confidence to join the Corps and marry my wife."

"Okay," Barney said. "Then if it was the game that gave you all of that confidence, why should you have to give it up? Have you decided where you're going to live when you leave the hospital? We'd like to keep you up here, but you're probably going somewhere else."

"Back to California, man," Carver said.

"Oh, La-La Land," Barney said a little sarcastically. "Well, wherever you live in the state of fruits and nuts, you'll find a team. Not as good as we are, I'm sure, but there'll be plenty of wheelchair hoopsters anywhere you choose to start a new life in California. When you get settled, call me. I'll give you all the information you need about how to order the right chair, along with a list of all the coaches and teams in Southern California. You know, Antwone, with your background, you might just have the makings of an Olympian."

"Olympian?" Carver said. "Olympics? What do you mean?"

"The Paralympics," Barney said. "Every four years, just like the regular games, and just as competitive. We have a couple of guys from our squad that are hoping to make the U.S. team. It's pretty awesome, man. Pretty awesome.

"Listen, I'd better make sure that none of the guys get into any trouble over too many beers. See that pouch on the side of my chair? Reach in there and get one of my cards. Remember, I'm not just the coach of this team; I'm a brilliant accountant if you ever need my help."

Carver took a card, and Barney held his eyes. "I want to tell you something before I go, Antwone. I believe sports is the best way for anyone to prove they can make it back in the world. The competitive stuff that you get involved with on a basketball court or in wheelchair tennis or any other game can create a big-time feeling for a person about what's possible. I know society can be pretty cruel, and a man in a chair has to figure out how he's going to make it in the world; but when you watch these people out here tonight and consider how they're living their lives, I think you have to feel that anything can be achieved if you want it enough.

"Okay," Barney said, smiling, "I've bent your ear too much already tonight. But there's one more important truth I want you to think about."

"What's that?" Antwone asked.

"Out here we have three classes of players, based on their disabilities, right?"

Carver nodded.

"And then there's me—a quad—and across the table there's

your friend, the doc, who's blind, with a beautiful wife and family. Here's the real deal, Antwone—the bottom line. Everybody in life has a disability. Some disabilities seem to be more complex or more profound than others, but everybody has the same choice: you can either live life fully, or you can live it feeling sorry for yourself."

Barney said good night and moved his chair expertly away, using his blow stick for steering.

On the ride home, Carver was quiet, but as they got close to the hospital, Brenden couldn't help it. He had to ask.

"So how do you feel, Antwone, about what you saw?"

"I've got a lot to think about," Carver said seriously. "This stuff is pretty heavy on my head, but that dude Barney is really cool. And he said some things to me that, well, that are really right on."

"Like what?" Kat asked, exercising her prerogative as Antwone's new best friend.

"Well, he talked about how everyone has a disability and that we all have a decision to make about how we're going to live."

"Do you think he's right?" Brenden asked, hoping.

"Maybe," Carver said as they pulled into the driveway. "Maybe."

A half hour later, Antwone Carver was alone in his hospital room, lying on his bed and studying the ceiling.

Could life really have meaning? he wondered. *Do I really have a chance to be worth something to Darla and to myself? These guys might be right. Maybe I need to find out.*

Taking a deep breath, he picked up his cell phone from the bedside table and dialed. When Darla answered, he said, "I love you, Darla. Please come to Seattle."

chapter nineteen

Darla Carver couldn't go back to sleep after Antwone's call. Hearing her husband say he loved her didn't surprise her. She knew how much he cared for her, but his invitation for her to come to Seattle as quickly as possible surprised her.

She went to the kitchen and made a cup of tea, sat in the living room, turned on the lamp, and wondered, *What does this mean? Has Antwone had a change of heart and wants to save our marriage? Is he telling me that he'll be coming home to San Diego to be with me? Has the therapy he's been going through with Dr. McCarthy and the rest of the medical staff made a difference in his perception of himself, and of us as a couple?*

Her brain was spinning, but she knew that she wouldn't get the answers until she was with Antwone. So at three in the morning, she called United Airlines and made reservations to go to Seattle two days later. She expected to be there for a while this time, and she knew she would have to talk to the principal at her school, who had told Darla that if she needed to go be with her husband, he would find a substitute for her until she came back. Then she did something that was uniquely Darla: she went to her closet and busied herself deciding what she would pack and what she would wear when she first saw Antwone.

HER MARINE HUSBAND WAS also sleepless after their phone call. For Antwone, the major question was how he and his wife would find their way back to being a normal married couple again. He decided that he would take the advice Dr. McCarthy had offered and read some of the materials he'd been given, along with looking at the videos the doc recommended.

He shook his head in the dark, realizing that the men and women he had met tonight were pretty amazing. Again the blind psychiatrist had been right. These remarkable people deserved his respect, just like his fellow Marines. Carver was glad to know that Dr. McCarthy would be with them to help them through the awkwardness of a new beginning.

As he thought of Darla, he longed to be with her, to touch her, to hold her and kiss her. And in a real moment of clarity, he understood that again McCarthy might be right. *There is much more to love than sex,* he thought. And what he felt for his wife was total love.

He felt as though he was waking up from a bad dream, and

for the first time since he was hurt in Iraq, he felt hope. There was a glimmer of hope out there with Darla, and Antwone Carver was beginning to believe it.

BRENDEN AND KAT HAD caught the last ferry home, and while Kat dropped off the babysitter, Brenden took Nelson for a walk in the dark. Day or night, it didn't matter to Nelson—or to Brenden, for that matter. Brenden was impressed that the big dog could guide him as well in pitch-black darkness as he could in the brightest sunlight. In fact, Brenden had noticed that the big animal seemed to be even more alert and more sensitive to issues of danger when they worked at night.

They never went very far on these evening walks; just enough for both of them to stretch their legs and for Nelson to take care of business. Brenden knew it wasn't particularly professional, but he was elated with the way Carver's encounter with wheelchair basketball and the people who played it had gone. Whatever the coach said had certainly affected the young Marine, and Brenden felt that he would be able to make substantial progress in their future sessions.

WHEN HE ARRIVED BACK home, Kat was still awake, and she surprised him when she said that he had a phone call.

"Who was it?" he asked.

"My new best friend," she said. "Corporal Antwone Carver."

"At this hour of the night?"

"That's right, Dr. McCarthy. Your patient wanted you to know that he called his wife and asked her to come to Seattle."

Brenden cheered softly, careful not to wake the kids. "That's great," he said. "Really terrific. It means he's beginning to invest in progress. Kat, we really have a chance to get this guy back on his feet—I mean, his wheels."

Kat laughed as she took off her makeup. "Great choice of words, Mr. Sensitive. But I know what you mean. It is terrific, Brenden. You're a great doctor, a great husband, and I love you. So now that I've removed all the war paint, give me a kiss."

Brenden leaned forward and kissed his wife, first on the eyes, then on the mouth.

Holding her face in his hands, he said softly, "You have a beautiful face. It's perfect."

"You can tell that?" she asked.

"You bet," he said. "I love to look at it every day." His fingers traced along the line of her cheek and down her neck and then began to wander, taking in the full beauty of her woman's body.

A FEW DAYS LATER, Brenden met with the medical team that had been working with Antwone Carver. His occupational therapist and physical therapist were present, along with the attending physician—not Dr. Jonathan Craig. There was also a career placement counselor, who would help Carver in his post-hospital adjustment, and a Marine captain, who would help navigate the complex paperwork necessary for Carver to begin to collect his well-earned disability compensation.

Brenden had called the meeting because he wanted to be able to act aggressively to facilitate Carver's discharge from the hospital if his time with the Marine and his wife gave him the confidence to believe the man was psychologically prepared to go home. Everyone in the room was delighted to learn that the psychiatrist was hopeful there had been a major breakthrough, and they all signed off, leaving the decision completely up to Dr. McCarthy.

Now the Carvers sat across from Brenden: Antwone in his wheelchair and Darla on a chair she had pulled up close to her husband. Brenden heard them hold hands and felt their nervousness as they began the conversation. He also sensed that they were looking at each other and not very often at him. *That's fine,* he thought to himself. *That's exactly where I want their eyes to be—on each other and on their path to a new life.*

"First of all," he said, "Darla, I am so pleased to meet you. Antwone told me you were beautiful, and even a blind guy can figure out that he was right."

He could tell she blushed.

"Thank you, Dr. McCarthy," she said. "As long as Antwone thinks so, that's all that matters."

Brenden heard Carver laugh quietly, with more than one note.

"You see, Doc?" he said. "I told you how special she was."

"Yes, you did, Antwone, and because of what you told me,

I want to suggest to both of you that love is the most powerful force any of us have in life. It can conquer any adversity, and I believe it can overcome any obstacle. Darla, if it's not too personal, please tell me how you feel about Antwone."

The young woman was direct, and Brenden was very pleased.

"He's my heart," she said without hesitation. "He's everything I want in my life. Antwone"—now she spoke directly to him—"I believe the doctor's right—that love can overcome anything, any problem. We can work at it together. That's what a marriage is all about. Isn't that true, Dr. McCarthy?" she said, looking for support.

"I said it was," Brenden told her, "and I meant it. Antwone—and I can understand this—has been focusing on the issue of sex, but I've tried to reassure him that couples can enjoy their sexuality, even with major spinal cord injury."

Carver spoke, and Brenden was delighted to hear what he had to say.

"Doc, you know those videos you told me about? I mean, the couples with"—and he said it appropriately—"couples with disability involved in making love? I watched the DVDs, man, and they were, you know, they were real encouraging. Darla told me she saw the same ones."

"I did," Darla added. "I know it may be different," she said, and she looked right at her husband again, "but I'm excited to find out. I'm excited to be with you, Antwone—to be your wife again, to be your lover."

Something in Darla's manner broke the emotional dam wide open, and Antwone Carver began to cry. Darla put her arms around him, and Brenden sat still, letting the feelings flow between them without interruption.

After a little while, Carver said, "I guess maybe I'm back in the game, Doc. I guess maybe I'm going to try."

Brenden reached across the low table between them and shook the Marine's hand. "That's what I was hoping for, Antwone. That's what our time together has been all about. But before we start getting your papers together to get out of this place, I do want to talk to you about something else, if that's okay."

"What's that?" Darla asked.

"Well," Brenden said, "Antwone and I have skirted around this subject, but now, with the two of you, I'd like to explore, at least in general terms, what Antwone might consider doing with the rest of his life. I mean his professional life. Have you considered that?" Brenden asked. "Have you given any thought to your future?"

"Not really . . . ," Carver said and then chuckled. "Even though you tried to push me to do it."

Their shared laughter gave Brenden confidence in Carver's continued path toward psychological healing.

"Well," Brenden said, "the thing is, with Darla working as a teacher, I think it's important, both economically and for your self-worth, that you begin to consider what you might want to do with your work life. You know, Antwone, in our time together some things have become really clear. I've figured out that there are three things you really care about. Darla is number one."

He heard the two young people hug each other again and waited a beat.

"And then there's basketball. That might be number two. And we can't forget about the Corps. When it comes to Darla, frankly, Antwone, I'm not really worried anymore, because I've felt the love between you and I know it's special. And talking about basketball, I think the other night you got a taste of a new game."

"Yeah," Antwone said. "The coach dude had something really interesting to say. He told me that when—what do I call them?—I mean, when normal people play the game . . ."

"That'll do, Antwone," Brenden laughed.

Carver went on, "When normal people play the game, it's a vertical game. Up in the air, you know? Above the rim. But when wheelchair people play, it's a horizontal game. What he told me was that I just have to get used to playing a different game."

"So how do you feel about that?" Brenden asked.

Carver laughed again with more than one note. "It's cool, man," he said. "Those guys can really play. You were right. They really can play hoop and rock."

"So," Brenden asked, "what about the Corps?"

"Listen, man," Carver said, "that's all over with. What are they going to do, create a brigade of wheelchair guys like some kind of Special Forces unit or something?"

"No," Brenden said, "but you know, Antwone, I had an interesting conversation yesterday with the recruiting office out of San Diego, and I learned something really exciting. The Corps is now employing wounded vets to sell young people on joining up."

"That doesn't make sense, man," Carver said. "Why would they hire shredded guys to talk young dudes into becoming Marines?"

"Because," Brenden said, "if some kid meets someone like you, and you're telling them that the Corps is a great life and that being a Marine is about the best occupation a person could have, how can they ever say you're wrong? Wounded Marines are the best poster boys for the service, and when I told this recruiter—here's his name and number, by the way . . ."

Brenden passed a card across the desk to Carver.

"When I told this recruiter about your background, he was really interested in you."

"Interested?" Carver asked. "In *me*? Why?"

"Because he told me that the Corps is looking for people who commit to it. They believe that their training and the way they develop loyalty and *esprit de corps* is exactly what lost kids are looking for."

"You mean like family," Darla said.

"That's right, Darla. Like family. Antwone has told me a couple of times that the Corps was like his family, along with you, of course."

"I believe that," Darla said. "You know, Antwone, when you put on the uniform and I looked at you, so handsome, all spit and polished, I could almost see the pride coming out from inside you."

"I guess it's true," Carver said. "The pride, I mean. I really do feel it."

"And it's still there?" Brenden asked. "In your heart?"

Carver tapped his chest. "Yeah, it's in here, Doc," he said. "Right along with Darla."

The woman leaned forward, and Brenden heard her kiss her husband lightly on the cheek.

"So when you get home, will you promise me you'll contact this guy?" Brenden asked.

"Okay," Carver said. "I'll talk to him. We'll see."

"Dr. McCarthy?" Darla asked. "When can Antwone leave the hospital?"

"As far as I'm concerned," Brenden said, "he can leave today. I met with your team this morning, Antwone, and they said as long as I'm comfortable releasing you, you can get your stuff together and check out this afternoon."

"For real, man?" Carver exclaimed, excitement in his voice.

"For real, Antwone. You know, you've been physically ready to leave here for quite a while now. We just had to get this other stuff together. So here's what I think. I told you when we first started down this road that as far as I was concerned, you were a hero—a hero to me, a hero to the Corps, and a hero to your country."

"And to me," Darla said. "To me first."

"That's right, Darla," Brenden said. "So we've been talking for a while, and we've learned a lot, and I think together we've grown a lot. On the card I gave you, if you check out the back, I've recommended a couple of doctors in San Diego, if you need to talk to someone. They're really good guys. I went to school with one of them, and I've called to let them both know you may be calling.

"The key to all of this, Antwone, is to remember what we said before. Everything comes in small steps, and you have to work at things one step at a time. We agreed that it's never easy, but I think now you finally believe Darla and me when we tell you that love is the most powerful medicine in the world. It's worth a lot more than anything that happens in therapy or with the medication that you take.

"And by the way, about that: because you're still on meds, you really do have to talk to one of my friends in San Diego. Most patients who struggle with PTSD are on the medication for a long time, and studies haven't yet concluded whether combat vets can do well without the help of the drugs. Frankly, we just don't know enough right now. So pick out one of those guys when you get home, talk to him, and don't be afraid of your meds."

"I'm already feeling better," Carver said. "It's amazing, but I really am feeling better."

"Well," Brenden said, smiling, "Darla probably has something to do with that, too, but I hope you'll keep me informed about how you're doing."

This time it was Carver who reached across the space between them and took the blind man's hand.

"I owe you a lot," he said. "Doc, I mean it. You saved my life, and I'll never forget it."

Now Darla was crying. "We won't forget it," she said. "Dr. McCarthy, you gave me back my husband, and that means you gave me back my life."

Brenden found himself beginning to choke up. "You know

what?" he told them. "When you do what I do, it doesn't get any better than this. Thank you for all you've given me, Antwone. We both got a lot."

They all stood, and so did Nelson.

"You were right about something else," Antwone said. "Growing up the way I did, I was always afraid of big dogs. But, Nelson," he said, turning to the big animal, "you're really cool, and your master is right. You're all about love."

The big dog moved in close to Antwone's chair and accepted a hug.

"Good luck," Brenden said as the couple moved out the door, "although I don't really feel you're going to need it. You have each other, and that is more than enough."

Carver looked at the tall blind man standing in the doorway, and out of either habit or respect, he snapped off a salute to the civilian and moved away down the hall.

chapter twenty

Manny Hernandez was tired, and not just because of the six days he and his crew had been working the nets in search of the halibut that should be far more plentiful at this time of year.

It was all different, he thought. So different than when he had been a boy and fished with his father, filling the freezers with a catch that was achieved in only half the time and half the distance.

His fuel cost had become absurd. *It's those foreign oil companies. They've got us right by the throat,* he thought, *and pollution is ruining the ocean. No fish.* On this trip, though he had gone all the way to the far banks, his hold was barely half full.

I'm nearly sixty years old, and I have nothing to show for it, he griped to himself. *My house is mortgaged all the way out. I've got loans on the boat, and nobody wants to buy her, even though she's the best troller in the harbor.*

She was called the *Mother Maria*, named after Manny's mother. He was Portuguese, from generations of fishermen dating all the way back to the founding of the New World. Manny was proud of his heritage, but right now he was bone tired, and all he wanted to do was go home to his Antonia, put his feet up, drink too much grappa, and forget about his troubles.

The fog was pea-soup thick. It had been a long time since he had come home in a fog like this. You couldn't see your hand in front of your face, but Manny had navigated these waters and this bay for over forty years, and he figured he could bring her in blind.

"Forget the five-knot speed limit. Take the shortcuts. Fifteen knots will save at least an hour."

BRENDEN WAS LEAVING WORK an hour early. Everything had gone so well with the Carvers that he decided he deserved to go home early, so he arrived at the dock for the four o'clock ferry, rather than the five.

He heard people commenting about the fog as they waited in line to board. He couldn't help but find it amusing listening to them. Fog meant nothing to him, and he knew from his nightly walks with Nelson that the big dog wasn't concerned about it either. Actually, Brenden had come to love the fog. He had learned that on nights like this, all of the sounds of life became compressed, heightened as they were held in by the thick atmosphere. For Brenden, the fog actually created more clarity, so it was a friend to the blind man and his dog.

Brenden loved the smell of the ocean when the weather was like this. The tangy richness somehow made him think about life renewed, and tonight that was what he was feeling. Antwone and Darla Carver were beginning a life of renewal, and nothing else in Brenden's professional experience had ever given him so much personal satisfaction.

So tonight he and Nelson would sit up top, out in the elements, for the short crossing to Bainbridge. From where he sat on the upper deck, the throb of the engines did not cover the sound of the foghorns that offered direction to incoming traffic. Brenden wondered if the crew of the ferryboat could see the lights of other ships through the fog, or whether they counted on radar and instruments to navigate the crossing. He had grown up in Colorado, so he actually knew very little about the ocean. That was probably why he was so enamored by the sea.

Sometimes he tried to picture the geography of his environment and how it related to the size and scope of the ocean. He realized that as the years went by, his ability to draw these dimensional pictures had diminished, even though his sensory acuity had increased.

It was like that with color, he thought. *There are a lot of shades I can't remember anymore, but it doesn't matter. The richness of all the things I've learned since I lost my sight far outweighs the subtleties I've lost.*

Getting up from the bench he was sitting on, he put his

hands on the ship's rail and drew in a full breath of the briny salt air.

"Terrific," he told Nelson. "Absolutely terrific."

He would be home in twenty minutes. Soon he would be hugging Kat and playing with his children and listening to all of them talk about their day, while he told them about the great one he had just had. He thought about what it was like to be an innocent child, with your mind so open to every experience life could offer and your brain not cluttered with wasted data built up over the years.

The other night his children had been asking about where things come from, with Brian saying, "When you turn on the light, Daddy, where does it come from?" and Mora adding, "When I want water, I just turn it on; where does it come from, Daddy?" *Good questions,* Brenden thought. And he smiled, remembering that he didn't really know the answers himself. What he knew for sure was that his children were innocent and beautiful, and he loved them.

He was thinking about his family when he heard the rumbling in the fog and realized that the noise was coming closer. Over maybe the next twenty seconds, he speculated about what it might be. It had to be another boat, but where was she going, and why was he hearing her engines coming so close? He started to tell himself that the ferryboat crew must know there was another craft out there in the fog, close on the port side. But before he could finish the thought, there was a crunching impact of collision, and the ferryboat's alarm bell sounded in the fog.

Months later, the investigation would find both the ferryboat captain and Manuel Hernandez grossly at fault. Hernandez had not obeyed either the speed limits or buoy markers in his haste to make port, and the ferryboat captain was found to have been on the outside, rather than the inside, of the marker that framed the appropriate lane of passage.

But that was months later. Right now there was a sickening grinding of metal on metal as the propellers of both boats continued to churn in the water, with the fishing boat's bow impaling the side of the ferry. Like a gigantic drill, the troller's engines were opening a gap right at the ferry's waterline, and the cold, hungry water of the bay surged in, swallowing up everything in its path.

Someone had the presence of mind to pick up the ferry's microphone and try to create order, instructing people to reach under their seats and put on their life preservers. But the impact had been so devastating and the damage to the ferryboat so complete that there wasn't time to take more appropriate action. She was listing hard with her bow down and was already beginning to sink.

Brenden heard the order to put on life preservers and was able to find his, though he found it difficult to get it on over his head. Nelson was bumping his master and whining, knowing that this was not normal; this was danger. People were screaming, especially those who had been sitting inside below deck.

Brenden could hear the sounds of scrambling feet and cursing as passengers realized they were trapped. It was a struggle for survival, and people were throwing each other out of the way as they fought to gain access to the staircases at each end of the ship.

Because the ferry's crew was made up of only five, there did not seem to be any semblance of command or control, and Brenden prayed that the people would somehow find their way out of the deathtrap below. He wasn't sure how much time had elapsed. It couldn't have been more than three minutes from the time of the collision, but already he was finding it difficult to stand. The boat was listing over at a dangerous angle, and he knew it wouldn't be long until he and Nelson had to go into the water.

He remembered how he had recently told the dog that it was too cold to swim. He figured that the water temperature must be around fifty degrees. People couldn't live in this water, he knew. Hypothermia and the weight of their clothing would take them down. Considering that, he began to strip off his clothes—his shoes and socks along with his pants and shirt—leaving him standing in the life preserver and his underwear. But at least he knew he would be buoyant. He wished—oh God, he wished—he could help some of the other passengers. If he were able to see, maybe he could do something, but he was a blind man with a dog on a doomed ferryboat, and all he could do was pray for his own and others' survival. And he believed God was listening, even though he continued to hear the screams of the people as some of them reached the upper deck. For some odd reason he thought of Antwone Carver, understanding what it must have been like for the Marine to listen to his friends' cries as they burned in the Humvee.

Now there were new sounds, as people began to leap into the sea. He knew that it was important to get away from a sinking vessel so that you wouldn't be sucked down in the vortex. He decided it was time for him and Nelson to join some of the others and try to save themselves.

"Okay, Nelson," he said to the big dog, "you and I are going to get that swim after all. Come on, boy. Come on."

Brenden leaned out over the railing, trying to feel whether it actually marked the edge of the boat or whether the decks below might protrude farther out. He wondered how far he would have to jump to clear any obstacles. He wasn't sure. And how would he make the dog understand what he wanted?

"I'm sorry, Nelson," he said, bending down. "We're going to have to do it this way, boy."

Brenden picked up the surprised animal and balanced him on top of the rail.

"Go, Nelson," he said. "Go on, boy. Jump." The dog turned his head back to his master, not understanding what he wanted.

"Go on, Nelson. I said jump."

Still the dog didn't get it, so, holding the animal on the railing, Brenden climbed up next to him, breathing hard. Taking the dog's collar in his left hand and reaching back with his right, he braced himself for a second on the edge and then pushed off into space, dragging the animal with him. The fall reminded him of going off the high board in a pool; maybe twenty feet to the water. But holding on to Nelson's collar and pushing off with his right hand, Brenden certainly was not aerodynamic; as they catapulted down, his trailing arm caught the side of the ship, and he heard the sickening sound of snapping bone as he and Nelson hit the water.

For a moment the shock of the cold numbed the pain in his arm and shoulder, but when it came, Brenden was overwhelmed by nausea. Nearly blacking out, he somehow found Nelson next to him—right where he should be—and locked the fingers of his left hand around the dog's harness handle. With his right arm useless, all he could do was keep his head above water and kick his legs. He fought back his own panic and reminded himself that the intelligent animal was still strong and capable. And would do anything for him.

"Nelson," he said, "take me home, boy. Take us home."

Swallowing salt water, he coughed and then spoke again to the animal.

"Let's go, boy. Let's go, Nelson. We've got to go home. Come on, Nelson."

Through the harness Brenden felt Nelson raise his head, then he heard him sniff the air, turning his neck from side to side as he worked to gain his bearings. The instincts of survival and home, developed over the years by dogs of all breeds, provided the black Lab with no doubt about what his master wanted and what he had to do to get there. After a few more seconds, he began to swim, dragging his injured master through the ocean's murky darkness.

The mayday call had gone out from the ferry within forty-five seconds of the collision, and five minutes later two fireboats, along with a Coast Guard patrol cutter, were moving. Though the fog was even thicker now, air-sea rescue also dispatched a helicopter equipped with a powerful Zeon light to aid in the visual search for passengers.

BRIAN WAS BUILDING WITH blocks, and Mora was playing with her dolls upstairs in her room.

Kat was preparing a salad for dinner while she watched the local news on a small television mounted in the kitchen. Though she was only half listening to the anchors, she nearly cut her hand with the knife she had been holding when she heard the female anchor say, "We have just been told that the Bainbridge Ferry has collided with an unknown craft. Coast Guard and fire rescue have been dispatched, and we're doing our best to stay on top of this developing story. At this moment we only know that it was the four o'clock crossing. The ticket manifest indicated a hundred and thirty-five passengers on board. Please stay with Eyewitness News for further details."

Kat stood frozen, her mind spinning. *When will Brenden be coming home? He normally takes the five o'clock boat. Will that be the case tonight?* She prayed he was only now leaving work, and she picked up the phone and dialed his cell. After three rings, the voice she loved came on the line.

"You've reached Dr. Brenden McCarthy," it said. "Please leave your name, phone number, and a message, and I'll call you back as soon as I can. And have a great day."

Kat's heart raced as she hung up the phone. *A great day?* She began to panic. Where was Brenden? Where was her husband?

She heard Mora talking to her dolls upstairs, and Brian called her, asking for help with his homework. *Life stops—life goes on,* she thought. *What to do?* She called a friend who lived two doors down.

"Annie," she said, "have you seen the news?"

"Yes," her friend said. "You're worried about Brenden. What can I do to help?"

"Could you come up and stay with the children for a while? I have to go to the docks."

"I know," her friend said. "I'll be right there."

BRENDEN WAS WILLING HIS legs to move, to keep kicking, to help Nelson keep him alive.

His brain was idly speculating whether the cold water was controlling the pain in his shoulder or just killing him. All he knew was that it was cold, incredibly cold. He knew about the swims that triathletes sometimes made—Alcatraz, for example, when the water temperature was in the high forties to low fifties—but the athletes were in wet suits. How long could you live in water like this before your body just gave up and you drowned? *Maybe an hour,* he thought.

But that wasn't true for Nelson, and Nelson was his hope. With Nelson, the question was his strength. How far would they have to go? Brenden didn't even know whether they were headed back toward the mainland or home to Bainbridge. He tried to remember how long they had been moving when the collision happened, and he decided they were about three quarters of the way to the island. Maybe that was the decision Nelson had made. He just didn't know.

He wondered whether he should have just gotten clear of the sinking boat and then stayed where he was, but the dog would not have understood; the only way for Brenden to move away from the sinking ship was to tell Nelson to take him home, and that's what the great animal was doing—pulling, pulling, pulling his master home.

Brenden could hear the dog's labored breathing as the animal struggled against the current. For a moment, Brenden considered releasing his friend from his burden by dropping the harness and allowing Nelson to survive on his own. He flashed back to the time, eight years ago, when he had been so overwhelmed by his sudden blindness that he decided to end his life by sitting down in the middle of a busy street. But Nelson had refused to let him die. The big Lab risked his own life to save his master's then, and he was doing it again now.

Then he heard it—a seagull's cry. He must be moving closer to the shore.

Had God placed these flying creatures in his life to act as angels? Moving him on a chosen path? He considered and shook his head in the dark. As the cold gripped him in its icy fingers, he willed himself to keep his legs moving, to survive, to live for Kat and their children.

In the distance, he began to hear a sound that at first he couldn't identify. What was it? He knew it, but he couldn't quite pull it into his tiring brain—and then he got it. It was the sound of waves breaking on the shore! They were getting closer to land; he could hear it.

"Good boy, Nelson," he croaked. "Good boy. Go on, boy. Go on. Keep going, boy. Take me home."

He felt the big animal reaching down inside for more reserves and somehow seeming to double his effort. The waves resounded in and out, closer and closer, and the big dog swam on.

Brenden felt his feet touch the rocky bottom, but he couldn't use them to walk. He was frozen—frozen stiff—and as the breakers swirled around him, he knew he was drowning. Water rushed into his mouth, choking him. He couldn't breathe, and he felt his grip on Nelson's harness loosening. The animal sensed it, too, and pulled even harder.

The water had become shallow, but even more dangerous, as sand found its way into his throat and lungs. He gasped for air and felt his head go under as a breaker rolled over him.

Nelson secured his feet on the ground and, with the Herculean effort of a sled dog, hauled his master clear of the surf.

Brenden lay on the mud, unable to move, but knowing somewhere in the back of his mind he had found land. He was safe. And somehow—thanks to Nelson—he would live.

chapter twenty-one

The man and the dog lay exhausted on the rock-strewn beach. Neither moved. Only the sound of their breathing—intermittent and ragged—suggested they were still alive. The man was conscious of nothing, had no idea where he was. Only the singular awareness that he was alive penetrated the cold and pain his body was experiencing.

The big animal, on the other hand, knew exactly where he was. He was on the island—their island. Only a few miles from home, and home was where Master had told him to go.

"Take me home," the man had said over and over again as they fought their way through the darkened ocean. "Take me home."

Nelson had brought them this close. Home was out there,

and as he gathered his strength, that was the thought dominating the animal's mind, consuming his being and committing him to the mission. *Get us home*. But how? How to get Master from the beach all the way home?

The animal licked the salt from Master's face and gently pulled on his arm, encouraging the man to get up, to move, to follow him. But Master was too hurt, too cold, too stiff to try.

Nelson needed water. He knew he needed it desperately. Dehydration was zapping his strength, and so the command "Take me home," along with the need for water, moved him to make a difficult decision. He would leave Master and go for help.

He was not the first animal to function in this way. The bond between dog and man had often been expressed in ways suggesting that these great animals' capacity to think, to interpret, and to understand was far more involved and far more significant than humans gave them credit for. And so Nelson moved off in the dark, headed for home and help.

THE BAINBRIDGE ISLAND DOCK was in chaos. Family and friends of passengers suspected to have been on the four o'clock ferry were gathering, trying to learn anything they could about their loved ones. The local Bainbridge police were there, along with some Coast Guard and paramedics from Seattle, the local chief of police from Parvo, and some annoying reporters who had commandeered a boat and arrived on the island.

Kat quickly realized that at this point no one knew anything for certain. There was a search under way, and Kat prayed that Brenden would be pulled from the water.

"Heavenly Father, please give Brenden the strength to survive. Keep him safe, and please bring him home to his family. His work is just beginning, and he still has so much to give."

For now, all that anyone knew was that the ferryboat had sunk and that survivors would be taken to a number of hospitals on the mainland. Though everyone wanted to make the crossing, the authorities had determined that only immediate family members would be transported.

Kat called Annie, and her friend promised that she would stay with the children overnight, and if necessary, get them off to school in the morning. Kat thanked her and was on the first boat making the crossing to Seattle, where she sat in the waiting room of County Hospital with all the others.

The minutes seemed to pass like hours. Just after midnight the paramedics started to bring people in, and Kat watched as the gurneys rolled by her; she saw every face, but not Brenden's. Not the face of the man she loved. Not the face that held her heart. Not the touchstone of her soul. Brenden was still out there somewhere in the bay. Alive or dead, he was out there with only Nelson to help him.

The fog had lifted, and morning was about to replace the night. The Bainbridge chief of police suggested that all of the families go home and get some sleep.

"We have your numbers," he said. "Honestly, there's no real reason to stay here. I mean . . ."

And he stopped.

"You mean there are no more survivors," a man said.

"No. No, that's not what I mean," the chief said, struggling for the right words. "But I think that it's important for all of you to try to get some rest."

About twenty people filed out of the hospital, representing the ten or fifteen families that were left. No one spoke during the cold crossing to Bainbridge. There was simply nothing to say.

For the first time that night, Kat began to consider what she would tell the children if—

She nearly choked on her tears, unable to go on with the thought.

"He's alive," she said out loud. "I know it. Brenden's alive. He's young and strong, and he's alive."

Arriving at the island, she politely thanked the policeman who offered to escort her home.

"I live right over there," she said, pointing, "just two minutes away."

As she walked toward the condo, for the first time in her life Kat Collins-McCarthy felt what it truly meant to be alone. The feeling of emptiness was completely overwhelming, and the devastation of the potential loss of her husband was so heavy on her heart that she thought it would break.

NELSON WAS HOME—OR almost home. Because Master's family lived on the upper floor in their building, the big dog couldn't get to Lady, couldn't feel Boy's hug, couldn't lick Girl's beautiful face. So he sat on the stoop outside, looking up and whining quietly. Then he felt her vibration. He had done this a lot when he and Master had been babysitting the children. Nelson always could tell when Lady was coming home; now the vibration was strong, and the animal stood on point, quivering, waiting for her to come around the corner of the building, signaling that he could run into her arms.

She cried out loud as the animal galloped to her. Dropping to her knees and hugging him, her tears fell on his salty coat as she held him, rocking him like one of her children. Lady was crying, and Nelson was whimpering, but the dog's cries carried more importance. He broke away from the woman and bounced back and forth in front of her, barking with a shrillness in his voice that said, *Listen to me. Come on. Follow me.*

Thank God she got it, and they both began to run. Kat was a good athlete, but now she ran with the desperation and adrenaline of a wife desperate to save her husband's life. Nelson was exhausted and nearly dying of thirst, but he ran on, driven by the same love Kat felt for Brenden.

LIKE KAT, BRENDEN MCCARTHY had never felt so alone as he lay on the beach in desperate pain, now without Nelson to comfort him. *Where did the dog go?* He understood that at some point as he drifted in and out of consciousness the animal had left him. *Why? Why is Nelson not here?* Could it be that they had washed up on the island? Could it be that his friend had gone for help? Brenden hoped so. He prayed so.

I wish I could move, but I'm so cold and so hurt.

NELSON HAD LEFT THE road, and the dog and the woman scrambled over sand dunes and rocky outcroppings to get to the ocean. Kat fell a number of times, banging her elbow and bloodying her knee, but she did not let up; eventually they arrived on a promontory just above the beach.

Nelson leaped from rock to rock as Kat eased herself down the side of the hill, her eyes straining, searching, and then . . . finding him.

"Brenden!" she cried. "Brenden!"

She was beside him now, holding his head in her lap, stroking his face, kissing his eyes.

"Brenden. Brenden."

With his good hand, he touched her face and whispered, "Don't cry, Kat. It'll be all right. Nelson took care of me. It'll be okay."

"Oh, Brenden," she said, still crying. "Oh, Brenden, I love you."

Pulling her cell phone from her pocket, she dialed the Bainbridge police, and a few minutes later the paramedics arrived, putting a sling on Brenden's shoulder and wrapping him in thermal blankets.

"We're going to medevac him," they told Kat. "We're worried about hypothermia. His body temperature is way down.

There isn't enough room in the bird. The police will get you to the hospital as fast as they can."

"Thank you," Kat said. "I'll get the dog home and then meet you there. Take good care of my husband, please."

"Will do," the young medic said. "You take care of that amazing dog."

The patrol car drove Kat and Nelson home, and after giving the big animal some water, she left him with Annie and the kids. Then Kat hitched a ride on a police boat back across the bay to the hospital.

When she entered Brenden's room in the ICU, she was greeted by a doctor going over his chart.

"Your husband's a lucky guy," the doctor said. "He has a dislocated shoulder, a broken humerus, a couple of cracked ribs, and maybe a puncture of the lung on the right side. There are some small abrasions and a couple of chipped teeth, but all in all, he'll heal."

"Thank God," Kat said. "Thank God."

Brenden was alert enough to try to smile.

"Hi, babe," he said. "I guess I'll be home for a while, and you'll be taking care of me."

"That's okay with me," she said, smiling. "That's just the way I want it."

The doctor turned and moved to the door. "I'll leave you two alone," he said. "Try to take it easy, Dr. McCarthy. You're pretty banged up, and what you need right now is rest."

After the doctor had left, Brenden said, "Do we know how many people were lost out there, Kat?"

"Twenty-two at last count," she said. "That's what the police told me."

Brenden sighed, taking in the news.

"Nelson saved my life," Brenden said, reflecting. "I wouldn't be here if it hadn't been for him. I hurt my arm and shoulder in the fall, and I don't know if I would have been able to survive in the water if Nelson hadn't kept me going. He put it all on the line for me, Kat. He risked his life. You know, during my therapy sessions with Antwone Carver, I talked to him about the Bible verse 'Greater love hath no man than this, that a man lay down his life for his friends.' That sure describes Nelson. It's the ultimate testimony of faith."

Kat squeezed her husband's hand, acknowledging a bond with God and each other.

Brenden went on. "So is he okay?"

"He's just fine," Kat said. "He was thirsty, and he's tired, but he's at home with the children, and Annie's with them. Brenden . . ." Her voice cracked, heavy with emotion. "Brenden, I don't know what I'd do if anything happened to you."

"I thought about that a lot, Kat," Brenden said, "out there in the dark. I thought about how much I love you. That's what kept me going. I just couldn't die out there, Kat. I love you."

They were quiet for a minute, with the woman sitting close by the bed, holding her husband's hand.

Finally he said, "Now I understand what Antwone Carver was talking about."

"What do you mean?" Kat asked.

"I mean, when the Marines talk about their Alive Day. You know, the day they beat death. They call it their Alive Day because for them it's about surviving and new beginnings."

"So this is your Alive Day," Kat said.

"Yeah," Brenden acknowledged, absorbing the concept, pulling it deep into his consciousness. "What's the date, Kat?"

"April 28th," she told him.

"April 28th," Brenden said. "My Alive Day."

epilogue

Nine months had passed since the sinking of the ferry, and Brenden's injuries had completely healed. He had returned to his morning ritual of exercise, and Nelson was guiding him better than ever.

Mora had started kindergarten, and Brian was a second grader, allowing Kat to substitute-teach in the local school system.

Christmas had been special for the McCarthy family, with Santa Claus still very much in the picture and Kat and Brenden making the most of their holiday experience. The new year had dawned full of promise and hope, and Brenden was even more grateful for every day of his life.

The phone rang in the middle of breakfast on a Saturday

morning in January. Immediately Brenden could tell that Kat was both surprised and delighted by the call.

"Antwone Carver," she said. "We think about you all the time. How is your lovely Darla?" She smiled at Brenden. "She's what? Oh my goodness, Antwone. You have to tell Brenden about this yourself."

Brenden took the phone from her hand.

"Okay, Marine," he said. "What's so exciting?"

"Darla's pregnant," Carver said. "We're going to have a baby, Doc. It's the real deal. We're going to have a baby."

"Antwone," Brenden said, "I couldn't be happier."

"And you know what?" Carver said, excited. "We learned about it yesterday, and you know what today is, Doc?"

"Saturday," Brenden said, sounding stupid.

"Yeah, dog, it's Saturday," Carver said, "but it's also my Alive Day."

"Oh man," Brenden said. "I forgot."

"It's my Alive Day," Carver went on, "and now Darla is pregnant. And that's not all. Remember we talked about my taking a job with the Corps as a recruiter?"

"Sure, Antwone," Brenden said. "That's what I hoped would work out for you."

"Well, it did," Carver said. "For the last two months I've been talking to brothers in neighborhoods all over California. So far I've signed up just over a hundred guys, and it feels great."

"So you really have a family now, don't you, Antwone?" Brenden said. "The Corps, Darla, and a new addition to your family."

"Listen," Carver said seriously. "I want to ask you something, Doc. If it's a boy . . ." He paused. "If it's a boy, would you mind if we named him Brenden?"

"Antwone," Brenden said, "I would be honored if there was a Brenden Carver in the world. If he's anything like his dad, he'll grow up to be a hero."

"Thanks for saying that," Carver said. "By the way, I got your letter a few months ago. The one that told me you had an Alive Day yourself. Pretty scary, huh?"

"I'll tell you something, Antwone," Brenden said. "I learned that you were right. When you have an Alive Day, you come to understand that each day you live has to be meaningful. That's what I feel all the time."

"You know what, Doc? Everybody should have an Alive Day, because it's what makes us know that living is what it's all about."

"You got it right," Brenden said. "Alive Day makes us know that living matters and each day has to count. I'll see you soon, Marine. Keep us posted on how Darla's feeling, would you?"

The men hung up and Brenden turned to his wife. "Let's make this a special day, Kat. Let's get the kids and do something really special. I want to celebrate"—he put his arm around his wife—"what it really means to be alive."

Dear Reader,

I'm delighted you've taken this journey with Brenden, Nelson, and Antwone. While the story started as an extension of my love for the black Lab named Nelson (a fictional version of a real dog I had for years) who was willing to lay down his life for his friend, it became a journey for me as I learned about the amazing women and men of our military.

While fictional, *Alive Day* shines light on a very real challenge facing our nation: that of truly welcoming home the heroes who fight for our country. Not just with banners and kind words—which are helpful, to be sure—but with real programs and tangible results. My hope is that you'll feel empowered by this story to fight for those who have served us so nobly.

Training for new careers, reentering civilian life, and coping with post-traumatic stress disorder are probably the most important issues facing veterans. Since Congress is attempting to write new legislation on veterans issues, most particularly payments for war injury, writing to your congressperson in support of veterans legislation remains critical.

I hope you'll join me in prayer and action to support these amazing men and women.

Peace be with you,
Tom Sullivan

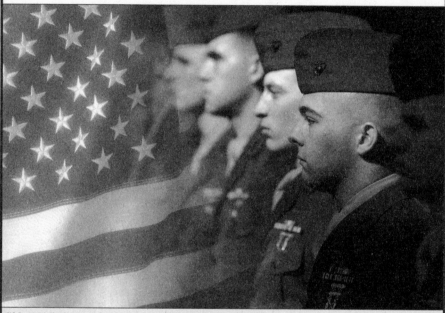

Love shared is more valuable than any other gift.

To find out more information, visit these Web sites:

Guide Dogs for the Blind	www.guidedogs.com
Leader Dogs for the Blind	www.leaderdog.org
The Seeing Eye	www.seeingeye.org
Morris Animal Foundation	www.morrisanimalfoundation.org

READING LOG
